THE
ELEPHANT
OF SURPRISE

BOOKS BY JOE R. LANSDALE

THE HAP AND LEONARD NOVELS

Savage Season
Mucho Mojo
The Two-Bear Mambo
Bad Chili
Rumble Tumble
Captains Outrageous
Vanilla Ride
Devil Red
Honky Tonk Samurai
Rusty Puppy
Jackrabbit Smile
The Elephant of Surprise

OTHER NOVELS

The Magic Wagon
The Drive-In
The Nightrunners
Cold in July
The Boar
Waltz of Shadows
The Bottoms
A Fine Dark Line
Sunset and Sawdust
Lost Echoes
Leather Maiden
All the Earth, Thrown to the Sky
Edge of Dark Water
The Thicket
Paradise Sky

SELECTED SHORT-STORY COLLECTIONS

By Bizarre Hands
Sanctified and Chicken-Fried
The Best of Joe R. Lansdale

THE
ELEPHANT
OF SURPRISE

JOE R.
LANSDALE

MULHOLLAND BOOKS

Little, Brown and Company

New York Boston London

Copyright © 2019 by Joe R. Lansdale

Hachette Book Group supports the right to free expression and the value of copyright. The purpose of copyright is to encourage writers and artists to produce the creative works that enrich our culture.

The scanning, uploading, and distribution of this book without permission is a theft of the author's intellectual property. If you would like permission to use material from the book (other than for review purposes), please contact permissions@hbgusa.com. Thank you for your support of the author's rights.

Mulholland Books / Little, Brown and Company
Hachette Book Group
1290 Avenue of the Americas, New York, NY 10104
mulhollandbooks.com

First Edition: March 2019

Mulholland Books is an imprint of Little, Brown and Company, a division of Hachette Book Group, Inc. The Mulholland Books name and logo are trademarks of Hachette Book Group, Inc.

The publisher is not responsible for websites (or their content) that are not owned by the publisher.

The Hachette Speakers Bureau provides a wide range of authors for speaking events. To find out more, go to hachettespeakersbureau.com or call (866) 376-6591.

ISBN 978-0-316-47987-5
Library of Congress Control Number: 2018963460

10 9 8 7 6 5 4 3 2 1

LSC-C

Printed in the United States of America

For Bill and Judy Crider. Good friends.
Gone, but not forgotten.

That's a lot of damn water.

Noah

Me and Leonard got something better than the element of surprise, we got the elephant of surprise, and you can bet that's some serious business.

Hap Collins

1

The night was dark, wet, and cold, and the rain was coming down hard. The trees on the right side of the road were bending toward us as we passed, and leaves and limbs were coming loose of them, tumbling in front of and against the car. I kept driving, dodging branches when I could, hoping there were no washed-out sections in the road or a limb didn't hang up beneath us.

The wipers slaved back and forth like a mean librarian wagging her finger at a loud child, and the lights bounced off the night. I kind of wished to see another car on the road, but most everyone else had sense enough to get in out of the storm.

Me and Leonard had finished up a surveillance job in San Augustine and were on our way back to LaBorde. When we'd left, the sky was clear and you could see the stars and the partial moon, but that situation had changed five miles out of town. First came the wind, then thunder and lightning, finally the rain, and then the wind picked up even more, and it began to seriously storm.

I had the car heater on to fight the January cold, and it was mostly working. I was hungry and thinking about being home with some food and a big hot cup of decaf coffee but knowing, late as it was, I ought to just go on and go to bed and wait for breakfast.

Maybe just a granola bar and a glass of milk.

Or I might have some cereal. Only one bowl. A small bowl. A bagel, no cream cheese. Light butter, maybe. Might be some of that barbecue left over from the other day. No. That was too heavy. But hell, barbecue, that was nice, and if it stayed in the refrigerator too long it could ruin.

Leonard said, "Look out, man."

I looked up as something ran into the highway. I whipped to the right, just missing a bar ditch, and skidded to a stop in a spray of water. I glanced in the rearview mirror and then the water-beaded side mirrors, but all I could see was rain.

"It was somebody," Leonard said.

"Could have been an animal?"

"It was someone," he said. "A girl, I think."

I drove up a space and turned in the road, trying to be careful not to end up too far on either side, as the earth there slanted down into ditches. It was wet and muddy and steep, and easy to slide. If we ended up in a ditch, it would be full of fast-running water and the only way out would be a wrecker, if we had cell service to call them. We were in a bad place for that. And I wasn't sure a wrecker service would come out in this. Hell, Noah wouldn't come out in this, and it was getting worse by the moment.

I got us turned around and drove slow but didn't see anyone, at least not at first, and then Leonard said, "Hap."

I braked and skidded slightly, looked where he was pointing. A girl stumbled back into the road, having made it across, then having decided to come back. She was waving her hands at us. Her hair was white in the headlights and was plastered against her head like a cowl, some of it draped across her face, and there was something dark running from her mouth and down her chin. The rain washed it away as fast as it appeared. She was small and pale and obviously weak. She was wearing a stained T-shirt and pajama shorts and was barefoot. She collapsed in the road.

Leonard got out and went after her, the rain hammering against him, the cold wind whistling into the car through the open door. He picked her up like she was a doll and carried her back to the car. I unfastened my belt, leaned back and stretched over the crack between the seats and worked the back door open. Leonard set her inside, nudged her to the center of the seat.

With the doors open, the inside was lit up, and I saw the girl was an albino, and Asian, and so small I at first thought she was a child of eleven or so. She opened her mouth and blood ran out and dripped over her chin and onto her chest. She looked up at me with pale eyes, not white, but a blue so thin they were almost clear. She had the appearance of a wounded bird trapped behind glass. She tried to talk but all that came out of her mouth was blood and a choking noise.

Leonard closed the front passenger-side door, slid in beside her on the backseat, closed the back door, said, "You're all right. We got you. Easy, now, let me look. Open your mouth."

He gently touched her chin, looked inside her open mouth, said, "Hap, give me the flashlight."

I reached over and into the glove box where we keep a pistol and a flashlight and some odds and ends and pulled out the flashlight and gave it to him.

The young woman was starting to moan.

"Easy," Leonard said, "just a peek."

Leonard looked, and there in the glow of the flashlight, I could see his face change.

"Give me the Kleenex," he said.

I opened the glove box again and got out a small packet of Kleenex. Leonard took it, tore the plastic cover off of it, pulled out all the Kleenex, and said, "Honey, you need to put this here in your mouth and close it gently. Might tilt your head back, but don't lie down."

He put the Kleenex in her mouth, and she didn't argue about it. He strapped the seat belt around her, said, "You'll be all right."

That's when a big black SUV came out of a side road about where the girl had first appeared and turned into our lane so that its headlights were pointing right at us. The SUV stopped and a big black man in black clothes wearing a dark, rain-beaten hat got out of the car on the passenger side. He looked as if he could straighten the Leaning Tower of Pisa with one hand. He had a large pistol held down by his side. The tower gave him any shit, he could shoot it.

I said, "Leonard, hang on."

The man in the road lifted the handgun.

2

I threw the car in reverse and looked over my shoulder between the woman and Leonard, and as far as I could tell, all that was behind us was night and rain and the faint glow of my taillights. I stabbed the gas and away we went. I heard a gun crack and something scraped across the top of the car. It had been a hasty shot.

I kept my foot punched down on the gas, took a forward glance, and saw that I had made quite a gap between us and the SUV, but a Prius isn't a race car.

Leonard said to the girl, "Hang tight, kid."

He slid between the seats and into the front, opened the glove box and took out the automatic pistol, said, "Turn it around."

I stepped on the brake and the car slid. I turned the steering wheel in the direction of the slide and whipped the car completely around amidst a spray of water and a moan of tires, a move that was aided by a wet road and a bit of experience.

I hit the gas and looked in the rearview mirror. Lights. They were coming, and they were coming fast.

For a moment, I thought about a side road but decided that was a bad idea. Then I considered the main road we were on and how fast they were coming, and that wasn't such a good idea either. The only way I could see out of this problem was levitation of the car, and believe me, I was really concentrating on that, hoping I would find within me unknown powers of telekinesis. But nope.

Leonard hit the window button, rolled it down, hung out of the window, and pointed the pistol at them. Leonard is a so-so shot, and with that handgun and the rain and wind being like it was, I felt he had about as much of a chance of hitting that car as he had of farting a bird off a tree limb.

He fired twice, rapid succession. I glanced back. The lights were still coming. They probably had no idea he had a gun. He fired twice more. The SUV went sideways and tried to straighten, and then sparks flew up from underneath it.

Leonard had somehow hit the front right tire and they were dealing with a blowout, the tire rim slamming on the concrete.

The SUV swerved and tried to slow, but it was too late. It was all over the place, and then it went sideways and the taillights tipped toward the sky. It had fallen into one of the long, wet ditches by the side of the road.

3

———

"Someone tried to cut her tongue out," Leonard said. "They sawed about halfway through it."

We were sitting in LaBorde Memorial Hospital, having brought the girl in before calling the cops. Our friend the chief of police, Marvin Hanson, was off on a trip with his family somewhere up in the wilds of Montana, and Leonard's boyfriend, Pookie, also a cop, was out of town, visiting his sister in New Orleans. The two cops who were there didn't know us as well as the chief and Pookie did, and I couldn't decide if that was a good thing or a bad thing. Way they were looking at us and talking to us, you would have thought we had tried to cut her tongue out ourselves.

After a while, they had the hospital open up the gift shop that had closed hours before, and we bought T-shirts and underwear and socks and windbreakers that all had hospital logos on them. In a bathroom, we squeezed our jeans out in the sink and dried them pretty well in front of the hand dryers and put on the clean underwear and socks. The jeans were still damp but not as miserable cold and wet as before. Leonard had been out in it when he picked up the girl, but just going from the car into the hospital, Leonard carrying the girl, we had both been soaked to the bone.

When we came out of the bathroom, the cops were standing there like they thought we might squeeze into the toilet and flush an escape.

We had to drive to the station and answer all the questions again. A matter of routine, they said. Sure, they thought we were Good Samaritans. Sure, they believed us. Cops believe you like they believe in Santa Claus.

They had already sent cops out to see if they could find the SUV in a ditch, and they had taken the gun Leonard used. We both had permits, so at least we had that going for us.

We sat there in the station in the interrogation room until a lady cop we did know, Manny, came back and said they had found the SUV. We were sure as hell glad to see her, but she stayed professional throughout. It was all being filmed, of course. That's how an interrogation room works.

"The SUV was there. But shooting at cars, Leonard, that could cause you some problems," she said.

"Figured getting shot by them might cause me some problems too."

Manny was her usual attractive self, but the long white scar on her cheek was whiter than usual against her otherwise flawless Hispanic skin. She had a look on her face like she had been dragged out of bed by a pack of wolves. I looked at my watch. It was two in the morning. Did wolves work that late?

"Tracking the plates, of course," I said.

"Already have," she said. "They belong to a family in Oklahoma, but they don't own the SUV the plates are fastened to. VIN number on the car is being looked at, but you know how that will turn out."

"The car will have been stolen or the VIN number will be a false one, something like that," I said.

"Bad night for those assholes to be out wandering around without a ride," Leonard said.

"Unless someone picked them up," Manny said. "I tried my phone there. There's service. You should have done that, called it in."

"No service where we first came across them," I said. "And we were a little too busy being chased by them to try and phone on down the road. Yeah, I should have worried about that instead of worrying about getting the girl to the hospital."

Manny gave me a hard look. "Fair enough, and I get it. Don't run it into the ground."

"Look, Manny," I said. "You know we didn't hurt that girl, and you know we had to do what we did. They shot at us. They were trying to get to her, for whatever reason."

"Poor girl," Manny said. "Who could do that, and why?"

"Humans," I said. "That's who."

"Any idea who she is yet?" Leonard said.

Manny shook her head. "No idea, but whoever she is, someone wants her to suffer and die, that's for sure. Maybe she gets where she can talk or write a little, we can find out. She didn't have identification on her. If she was from these parts, someone would know her. Not that many albino girls around."

"Listen here," Leonard said. "Whoever did that will most likely still be looking for her. Best you have someone in the hospital to watch over her."

"How would anyone know she's there?" Manny said.

"That's an easy one," I said. "Where else would a rescuer take her?"

"Good point. I don't normally make the decisions here, but it's me for the night or until Marvin gets back. Wait a moment."

Manny went out.

After a bit, she came back. "They're posting someone at her door," she said. "He's already started over. Good cop, Eric Braider."

That was a relief. Probably unnecessary, but you never knew for sure.

Finally, they let us go with warnings not to leave the state. We drove to the IHOP at the end of North Street and had a late-night supper and breakfast. I had a short stack and Leonard ate enough pancakes, sausages, and eggs to feed an army and most of their relatives.

"Who would do such a thing to a little girl like that?" Leonard said, asking what had already been asked.

I didn't have an answer.

Outside, the rain slammed the parking lot and rattled the windows. We had just finished eating when the lights went out.

We sat there silently, and after a while a waiter came over with a flashlight and told us he was sorry, but they were going to have to have everyone pay up and leave.

Since the register didn't work without electricity, there was a tedious time when we stood in line and people paid with cash or their credit card numbers were written down. Leonard gave them the ticket with two twenties and we left.

The rain and wind were so bad we could hardly make it to our car. Once we were inside, this time with Leonard driving, he said, "Think we ought to go back to the hospital. Not long until morning anyway. We can see how the girl's doing. Jesus, why would they do that to that girl?"

He kept coming back to that, and I still didn't have an answer.

"I no longer wonder why people do horrible things," I said. "I just know a lot of them do."

"Speaking of that, I like to be ready for those horrible people. I have another pistol under the front seat. Find it and put it in the glove box? Makes sense to have it in a more reachable position."

4

———

Lights all along the street were out, and we were once again the only car on the road. It was as if we were in an old science fiction movie and everyone had been killed or was in hiding because bad aliens had taken over the Earth.

"Did you know LaBorde is the barbecue capital of Texas?" I said.

"I don't give a shit," Leonard said.

"They have a blueberry festival here too."

"Who doesn't? I live here, Hap. I know that shit. Hey, this isn't the barbecue capital of Texas. Barbecue here mostly sucks."

"I'm just trying to pass the time with interesting conversation."

"It's not that interesting when you make it up."

"Boy, are you in a mood."

"You should have seen that poor girl's tongue," Leonard said. "They almost cut it out."

I was glad I hadn't seen it. "My jeans are dry," I said.

"Will you shut up?"

It took us an impossibly long time to reach the hospital. The lights were on there. Backup generators, I presumed. That would seem right for a hospital. But not all the lights were on, and some were not that bright. We went and sat in the lobby in the comfortable waiting-area chairs under dim lights. Leonard began to snooze, and then he began to snore softly.

Except for a middle-aged lady at the desk, we seemed to be the only ones in the hospital.

I pulled out my cell and called Brett, told her what had happened, told her we'd be home when we got home.

"Still have lights here, but it's scary out there," she said. "Chance and Reba and Buffy Dog are here with us. We had dinner and then they couldn't go home, or didn't want to."

"They're safer there. Did Reba eat you out of house and home?"

"Just complained about the food. She wanted McDonald's. I told her she was free to go to town and buy us burgers."

"Bet that shut her up."

"Nope. She said give her the money and the car keys and she'd go."

I laughed. Reba was a smart-ass kid we had kind of rescued. She lived with my daughter, Chance, and Buffy the Biscuit Slayer, also known as Buff, Buffy Dog, or the Buffinator.

16

Brett said, "Will the girl be all right?"

"I don't know. I think so. They sewed her tongue up, gave her some pills. She's sleeping upstairs."

"Poor thing," Brett said.

We passed a few more words and closed out the conversation. I turned to ask Leonard if he wanted to call his boyfriend, Pookie, but he was still asleep. Probably best not to call Pookie and ruin his out-of-town visit. Nothing he could do right then.

I put the cell away just as I saw a large tree limb tumble across the parking lot at the side of the hospital and slam into a car hard enough I could hear the impact. At least it didn't set off an alarm.

The wind began to howl and the rain became even more fierce. Lightning cracked and thunder rumbled, shaking the glass in the hospital windows.

I could envision, somewhere out in the Gulf, a vicious, unseasonable storm, perhaps a hurricane, sending in its reserve troops, giving us a taste of what it could do just to remind us that compared to nature, we weren't as important as houseflies.

5

When I awoke in the hospital waiting area, I checked my watch. It was seven in the morning. Leonard was still asleep. It was dark as night, and the rain and wind hadn't let up an ounce. In fact, it looked worse out there. Meaning there was nothing to see but absolute blackness. The sun wasn't going to shine that morning, maybe not all day.

The same middle-aged lady was at the front desk. I went up there, said, "You certainly are putting in the time."

She smiled at me. She looked weary.

"I'm supposed to be gone," she said, "but the rain is so bad I'm better off here in the hospital than on the road, and my replacement is better off home. I figure before the day is done, we'll have a lot of new occupants. A storm like this, it makes things crazy. If only the rain would stop. Better yet, the wind."

"Lady we brought in last night. When can we check on her? We were told she's in a room on the third floor."

"No visiting hours yet, but way things are, it gets nine, you can go in, unless there are any medical concerns."

I thanked her and sat down again, and that's when I saw a big man come in the front door carrying a long, damp cardboard box. He had it tucked up under one arm. He wore black clothes. He had a black plastic rain cover over his hat.

I recognized the man from his size. It was the big black man that had gotten out of the SUV with a pistol. He was even bigger than I'd thought, looked like a weight lifter, not a bodybuilder, kind of guy who could dead-lift a battleship. His face was as expressionless as a mannequin's.

He hadn't seen us last night, had seen only my car, maybe a shape hanging out of the window firing at the SUV, so he had no idea who we were. He hardly gave us a glance. He adjusted his hat with a touch of his hand and walked past us and the desk, toward the elevator. I had a good idea what was in the box.

The lady behind the desk might've thought about saying something to stop him, but she didn't. Not the way he looked. She just watched him pass. I thought that was most likely a good choice.

6

I shook Leonard awake, said, "Hey, the guy that took a shot at us just walked in."

"What?"

"He's over by the elevator. Had a long cardboard box with him. I don't think it was curtain rods."

"Damn." By that point he was on his feet. We both headed toward the big man as he stepped into the elevator, but moments later the doors closed.

We went back to the desk, but the woman was gone. A bathroom break, maybe. We couldn't just hang out and call the police for backup. By the time they got here, it would be too late. That guy was there to finish the job he and whoever he was working with had started.

"How would he know where to go?" Leonard said.

"This is the logical place for her to be. Phones here work,

so he called and convinced someone who didn't know any better to give him her room number."

I heard the front hospital door slide automatically back, and I saw another man enter. He was short and thin and white, wearing black clothes. He had a hand in his coat pocket, a bandage across his forehead, and he walked with a bounce.

Leonard saw him too.

We didn't wait to figure him out. We made the stairs before he made the elevator. "I think those two may be an unmatched set," Leonard said.

We charged up the stairs to the third floor, where the girl was, trying to beat the elevator. There was supposed to be a cop up there, and the thought of that was some relief. I hoped he hadn't decided to drift off or take a bathroom break.

When we got to the third floor and rushed out into the hallway, we saw the cop in a chair. He was a young, curly-headed white guy. He was posted about midway between us and the elevators, next to the girl's room. He was sitting up straight in the chair, his uniform crisp and his badge shiny. He had his hand resting on the butt of his pistol. He looked as alert as a hungry cobra.

The elevator dinged.

We rushed toward the cop. He had seen us around, knew we had brought the girl in, so he wasn't overly concerned.

"Guy in the elevator," I called out. "He's got a gun."

The cop stood up, looked puzzled.

I said what I had said again.

The elevator door opened before we could reach the cop and the girl's room.

The elevator was empty.

"Shit," Leonard said. "He got off on another floor."

I thought, Yeah, that would be an idea. He didn't know us, but he might have suspected protection for the girl, and since I'd stood up as he headed to the elevator, he might have assumed I was part of a protection detail.

In a way, I was, but I'd been doing a piss-poor job, and Leonard had been napping.

"What's going on?" the cop said. We had reached the door to the room he was protecting.

"Someone has come for her," I said.

That's when the big man came around the corner. He must have gotten off the elevator on a lower floor, used the stairs on the opposite side we had taken. The gun was no longer in a box; it was a shotgun, twelve-gauge was my guess. He handled it with familiarity.

The cop pulled his gun. Leonard pushed the girl's door open and went inside as I ducked down and the shotgun ripped. The cop, gun in his hand, lost his head, so to speak, and I was peppered with brains and blood and falling shot.

As the poor cop fell, his handgun slid back toward me, our only lucky break so far, and I grabbed it, darted inside the room as another blast from the shotgun splintered the wall and pocked part of the door.

Once I was inside, the door swung shut. There was a small

square of glass in the door and I saw the man fill the space on the outside. I flicked the door latch and scuttled backward with the cop's gun tight in my hand. I knew then how those three pigs felt when the wolf came to their door.

I took a quick look behind me. The girl was in the hospital bed. She was unconscious, probably drugged into peaceful sleep. Leonard snatched up a chair and swung it against the large, wide window, but the window held its own. He swung at it several times, but the chair kept bouncing off it.

I saw the big man push his face to the glass in the door. I jerked the gun up and fired and the door glass shattered. He had seen me move and had moved himself, and just in time. He moved fast for being about the size of the Statue of Liberty.

I turned, said to Leonard, "Stand aside."

I shot a hole in the big outer window, heard it crack; the cracks started at the hole and spiderwebbed in all directions. Leonard hit the window with the chair again. It finally fell apart with a crunch and a tinkle of falling glass. The cold wind and rain blew in.

"Watch for that motherfucker," Leonard said.

I glanced back at the door. I didn't see the man. I didn't see his shadow. I felt the cold wind and rain dampening my back.

I looked over my shoulder at Leonard.

Leonard set the chair down beneath the window, turned to the bed, jerked back the covers, lifted the IV bag off the IV stand, dropped it on the girl's chest, and picked her up. All she wore was a hospital gown, not the best clothing for the outdoors, since your naked ass hung out of the back of it, but it might beat dying in bed.

Holding her close to him, Leonard put his foot on the chair he had placed beneath the window and then stepped out into the swirling storm.

7

The shotgun roared and the wood in the door jumped apart, made a gap large enough to ride a donkey through. That guy was packing some serious ammunition.

I hurried to the window. The wind and rain pushed at me. My hair and clothes were soaked in an instant. I trembled in the cold. There was a wide ledge beneath the window. Not something you'd want to have a pachyderm walk, but wide enough. I could see Leonard moving on it like a tightrope walker, one careful foot in front of the other, carrying the girl, going away as fast as he safely could. The ledge might have been wide, but it was wet as a snail trail.

I turned and looked at the door. Nothing yet. The big man was being cautious, now that he knew I had a gun.

I stepped up on the chair and went after Leonard, nearly

losing my footing immediately. It was actually slimier than a snail's trail.

I put my back to the wall and inched along. Leonard made the corner of the building and turned out of sight. Carrying a girl, even a small one, walking on a ledge with a wet wind blowing hard enough to roll an army tank was no small feat.

What the fuck was he, a mountain goat?

I turned my attention back to the window. The gun was in my right hand, and I held it across my chest, kept my left hand down and against the wall, kept scooting.

The man stuck his head out the window. I snapped off a shot, and I could tell from the way the blood jumped like a dark arrow into the night that I had hit him. But I knew too that I had just parted his hair, because his hat jumped off and the wind caught it and carried it away. Had it been the shot I had hoped for, he wouldn't have been able to pull back.

I turned the corner around the edge of the building, crossed in front of one window and then another, and finally the ledge widened. Down below I could see another roof from a building that had been added on at some point.

That's when I caught up with Leonard, standing with the girl held tight to him, looking down at the roof below. It was at least a twelve-foot drop, and there was a lower concrete roof below us to another building, but it didn't look inviting.

I yelled out, "Don't do it!" but the wind snatched my voice and hauled it away.

Leonard looked down at the lower roof for a moment, then turned and continued along the widened ledge. I was moving along faster and caught up with them. When I did, Leonard said, "What now?"

I looked where he was looking. The ledge continued around a corner, but the question was, how did we get off of it without taking a swan dive? The best we could do was keep moving around the hospital.

There was a window near us. I said, "Hang on."

I pointed the pistol at the window and hoped no one's bed was right under it, that a nurse wasn't standing there doing something or other. The room was dark, so I figured the latter wasn't likely. I shot at the window, and it cracked. I leaned against it, and then I kneed it, and when I did, it gave and shattered and fell apart into the room. I felt a sharp pain in my knee but nothing to write home about.

8

The hospital room was empty, but it wouldn't take long for the big man or the little guy we had seen downstairs to find us. Not if they were serious, and I had a feeling they were.

I went over and locked the door, looked around the room.

There was a wheelchair folded up near the wall. The room smelled of disinfectant.

Leonard placed the girl on the bed and looked in the closet. There was another ass-open gown in it, like the one she had on, and nothing else.

"I need something to fight with," he said.

"Might I recommend a chair."

There was one by the bed. Leonard went over and got it and held it by the backrest.

"What we got to do is get her out of here," Leonard said.

"I'm just waiting for our gyrocopter to show up."

The copter didn't show, but a shape appeared at the busted-out window. It wasn't the big man. It was the little man we had seen come in downstairs with the bandage on his head, most likely covering an injury from the SUV taking a dive. He was stone-faced and wiry and had his hair cut so close to his head, he might as well have gone on and shaved it. His coat flapped in the breeze.

I lifted the revolver, but he sprang across the room like a kangaroo on crack, kicked me in the chest, and drove me back against the wall, sending the revolver skittering across the floor.

I was scrambling to my feet as Leonard swung the chair at him. He swung it low, but the man dropped down so quick, and was flat on his belly so quick, it was like he had turned into a snake. As the chair passed over him, he leaped forward, grabbed Leonard by the windbreaker with one hand, and used the other to hit him with a hammer fist in the forehead. I think he was going for the nose, which would have been smarter, but Leonard lowered his head a little, and just in time.

If Leonard's forehead hurt the little guy, he didn't let on. He grabbed Leonard's windbreaker with the other hand, swiveled, and threw Leonard over his hip, threw him so well and so high, Leonard's feet nearly touched the ceiling; a foot or so higher and he might have needed an oxygen mask. Leonard came down on the tile floor with a smack so loud, I felt the pain myself, felt it crawl up my ass and up my spine and come to a throbbing rest at the base of my neck.

I was on the guy by then, delivering a front kick to the side of his leg, but he moved, swung his leg out of the way and up, hook-kicked me in the temple. I was surprised to find myself on the floor.

As I tried to get up, he kicked at my throat, but I was able to throw a hand up and merely get my palm whacked, but that was no walk in the park either. It hurt so bad I considered gnawing my hand off at the wrist.

Leonard, who I thought might be napping, had recovered and was up. He leaped on the little guy from behind, wrapped his legs around his waist, hooked his heels into his thighs, threw his arms around his neck, and fell backward with the guy trapped between his legs.

That didn't last long. The little guy squirmed out of Leonard's grip so fast and so clean, it was like he was part eel. He recovered his footing and kicked out at Leonard, who was still on the floor.

I found the pistol, but by then the little guy had produced one of his own. It was going to be which of us could pull the trigger faster. Or that would have been the case, but Leonard stepped in with the chair again, knocked the little man's hand down. The gun went off and the shot hit the floor and bounced against the ceiling, went on up through the thin tiles. The gun itself was knocked from his hand.

By then the little guy knew it was time to leave. I had the gun, and he had air. He pulled his injured hand against his chest, scooped his dropped pistol up with his good hand, backpedaled gracefully, as if he always went places walking asswards.

He made the window, threw up a leg like a back kick, and set it on the ledge without even looking. Then he pushed off on his other leg and was suddenly standing on the ledge, looking in the wide space where the window had been. He grinned at us. I was going to try and shoot again, but Leonard fucked that up. He stepped into my line of fire and threw the chair.

It was a good toss, though. It hit the grinning asshole right in the face and knocked him off the ledge.

"Bingo," Leonard said.

9

Not quite bingo," I said.

The little guy's hands were clutching the ledge.

"Goddamn monkey," Leonard said.

He wide-stepped toward the window, and as the little man lifted himself up and his face rose into sight, Leonard smacked him one with a good straight punch. The little man's head went back, but still he clung. Leonard slammed his fist down on the little man's right hand, striking the fingers.

That made the little man jerk that hand free of the ledge, and when Leonard hit his other hand, his fingers loosened and he fell.

I ran over and leaned out of the window with Leonard. The little man had taken that twelve-foot drop like a cat, had landed on his feet and was crouched down, looking up.

The rain was washing blood from his face where Leonard had busted his nose. He grinned at us.

I leaned out with the gun and took a shot at him, but he was already moving, went over the side of the lower roof like Spider-Man.

"Where the hell did he go?" Leonard said.

"The ledge below, if he didn't miss his footing."

"I'm sure he didn't."

We pulled back into the room. I pushed the handgun into my windbreaker pocket, said, "Leonard, we'll put her in the wheelchair."

Leonard went to pick her up while I pulled the chair away from the wall and unfolded it. Leonard brought her over and gently placed her in the chair, giving me a glimpse of her naked ass, the color of the moon on a clear summer night. He arranged the IV bag so that it hung on the back of the wheelchair. I wasn't even sure if what was in it was getting into her.

I grabbed a blanket off the bed and threw that over her to give her some warmth and some dignity.

I sidled over to the door, pulled out the pistol, and peeked through the small glass square. Lot of darkness in the hallway. The little guy didn't stick his eye against mine. The big man didn't blow my head off with a shotgun.

I unlatched the door and opened it, stepped gingerly into the hall, listening to my heart pound.

Leonard pushed the wheelchair into the hall. The wheels squeaked a little.

"Maybe if we use the elevator, that'll fool them," I said. "They might not expect that."

"Why wouldn't they? They might also expect the stairs. Only thing they wouldn't expect is someone to drive a tank through the wall and evacuate us."

"We're on the third floor."

"We'll have to use the elephant of surprise. I'll punch the elevator down, but we'll take the stairs. You lead with the gun. I'll lift the chair and carry her down. She's light as a feather."

Leonard went to the elevator, pushed the button. By then I was turning down the stairs, the gun pointed in front of me.

10

With my heart still beating like a drum, I moved carefully. I had gone down one flight and was on the second-floor landing when the auxiliary lights went out.

I assumed someone had gotten to the backup generators, reasoning that if it was dark, we might not find our way so easy, but whoever it was hadn't considered my trusty cell phone. I took it out of my pocket and—

The battery was dead.

Shit. I put the phone in my pocket.

I put my hand on the railing and eased along until I had nearly made the bottom of the stairs. If it was like I thought, one of them would be waiting at each stairwell. The elevator was near one set of stairs, so whoever was there would have that covered. No matter which way we came down, they had us trapped.

I thought for a moment, then started up the stairs again. I met Leonard carrying the wheelchair with the girl in it.

"Turn around," I said.

We went back up, me helping Leonard lift the chair. On the second-floor landing I told him what I thought.

"Yeah," he said, "that's how I'd do it if I was them."

"But you'd think to bring snacks."

"Of course."

The girl hadn't moved. She could have been on Mars or at the bottom of the Grand Canyon for all she knew.

"I got an idea," I said. "Stay here."

There was a large trash can at the far end of the hall. I padded down there and picked it up. It was a little heavy, but right then, scared as I was, I had adrenaline strength. When I got to Leonard, I let the can rest on a stair step.

"Look here," I said. "Follow close with her, and when it starts, you push her like you're jet-propelled."

"All right," he said. "But what's the plan after that?"

"Push her toward the front door, but wheel around the desk and head for the side door to the parking lot."

"That's not much of a plan. Front door's closer."

"It works electronically. My guess, that generator went dead, so did the door. It's locked up for the night. Go out the back emergency exit, it's just a push-bar door. And hey, maybe they won't expect it."

"And maybe they got people waiting out there."

"Maybe they don't."

40

"Maybe shit don't stink if the wind blows just right," Leonard said. "That plan sucks."

"It's what we got."

"What say we push her into a closet and try to take out these guys by ourselves, without her being in the line of fire?"

"A closet?"

"She won't fit in my pocket."

"I don't know, man. We get killed, then she's in a closet somewhere. They could kill us and still find her. If we don't have her, they know she's somewhere in the hospital."

"Yeah, there's that," Leonard said. "Okay. This plan of yours is going to be back to our usual elephant of surprise, I suppose?"

"I don't know how large an elephant it's going to be, but if you mean half-assed but energetic, then yeah. But I got a little something in mind."

"In case things go south, nice knowing you, bro."

11

I stood at the bottom of the stairs with my trash can, leaning slightly against the wall. I could see through the gap leading off the stairs and into the main hallway. The lady who had been behind the desk was now on the floor near the front door. Blood was flowing out from under her head. Probably shot her so she couldn't get away and bring help. Poor lady.

That meant at least one of them was downstairs again, as we'd suspected.

I somehow lifted the heavy can above my head without it crushing me flat like an accordion and tossed it as hard and as far as I could. It hit the floor and bounced. A shotgun roared and the can jumped and the lid snapped free and trash popped out.

With the gun drawn, I stepped into the hall, turning in the direction from which the shot had come, thinking, Little Guy, don't be behind me, and I fired at Big Guy, who I could see standing, the shotgun lowered now, a look that might possibly pass for surprise on his face.

My shot hit him in the chest and knocked him down. Behind me I heard Leonard, who had been creeping down the stairs with the girl in the chair, rolling the wheelchair out of the stairwell and into the lobby. The wheels squeaked as he went. He swerved around the lady on the floor and charged past the desk toward the hallway and the rear exit.

I kept the gun on Big Guy. I went over and grabbed the shotgun he had dropped, saw him twitch a little, open his eyes, start to get up. I realized he was wearing a bulletproof vest. As he moved, the now-flattened slug I had fired rolled off his chest.

I should have shot him again. But I had his gun and we'd gotten the girl, so I figured we were ahead for the moment. No reason to kill someone if I didn't have to. Instead, as he put his hands and knees under him, I kicked him under the chin. It was like kicking a concrete block, but he went down again, rolled over on his back, twitched like a dying carp, then quit.

I put the pistol into my coat pocket, backed away from him holding the shotgun. I glanced at Leonard, saw him galloping toward the side door, pushing that chair.

I ran after them. Leonard wheeled the girl around and hit the door with his back; the door popped open, and out he went. I was exiting after them, pushing the door as it started to close, when a big blast of power hit it. A bullet. It had whizzed over my shoulder and torn a hole in the door about the size of a cabbage.

I ducked and wheeled back the way I had come. It was Big Guy, up and ready with a revolver about the size of a howitzer in his hand. I should have killed him when I'd had the chance. Leonard would have.

I cut down on him with the shotgun, but he was way down the hall and already moving to the side and behind the reception desk. Damn, he was swift for someone so big. I heard my shot rattle against the elevator.

I backed against the press bar of the door and went out into the parking lot, the chill wind howling and limbs and debris flying around me. I felt like I was in Dorothy's tornado.

Leonard was at the car, practically bouncing up and down on his toes. I knew why. I had the key in my pocket, if "key" is the right term for it; you have to indulge us older folks with all this new electronic equipment.

I reached them and touched the door and it automatically opened, needing only for me to have the key in my pocket. We got the back door open and got the girl slid into the seat. Leonard hung the IV bag on the laundry hook above her door. Outside, he popped the hatch up, folded the wheelchair, and put it inside. Part of it stuck over the backseat. That was all right. The girl didn't have to worry about headroom. She was asleep on the seat, blissfully unaware of all that was going on around her. You couldn't have stirred her with a brass band and a pack of howler monkeys.

While this went on, I was facing the emergency door with

the shotgun. It was a good piece between us and it, but not as far as the hallway shot had been.

No one came out.

I eased around to the driver's side as Leonard slipped into the front passenger seat. When I got in, I gave him the shot-gun, then I started the car and rolled down our windows so we could use our weapons if we had to. The cold and the rain blew into the car, but right at that moment, I found it refresh-ing. I was all het up.

I took the handgun out of my windbreaker pocket and put it on the seat between my legs. Leonard poked the shotgun out the window, said, "Show a head, you sons of bitches."

I pulled out of the lot, and when I reached the street, I had only one way to turn. To our right was a tree that was old and thick when Davy Crockett passed through this area on his way to his fate at the Alamo. It had been uprooted by the storm and fallen across the road, blocking an exit that way.

I turned left and started down the street through a whirl-wind of leaves and limbs, dirt and rain.

I felt relieved for about ten seconds.

In the rearview I saw a car come sailing out of the lot and turn after us. It was a big white Lincoln. I didn't think it was a coincidence someone else from the hospital had decided to leave and come in our direction at a high rate of speed.

"Haven't these assholes got something better to do?" Leonard said.

"Apparently not," I said.

Then I saw the street ahead of us was blocked. Two cars

had smashed together at some point, and the drivers had abandoned their vehicles.

I said, "Hold on to your ass," jerked the wheel right, and hit the curb. The Prius bumped over it with all the grace of a tricycle going over a railroad tie.

Into the yard we went. The tires spun in the grass, dipped into the soft earth, and for a minute, I thought we were screwed and double screwed.

Then the tires caught and the Prius moved. We bumped over some rough spots, hit a driveway, and then I turned back into the street, just beyond the cars that had blocked the road.

Now we had something of a clean run, at least as far as I could see in the headlights. Leonard turned in the seat and looked behind us and laughed.

"What could be funny?"

"They're stuck in the yard," he said. "That's what's funny."

"Okay," I said. "That is amusing."

Our bad luck held. We got to the end of the street and another large tree had fallen across it.

Simultaneously we both said, I think appropriately, "Damn."

"Go through the yard," Leonard said.

I looked at the yards on both sides of it. Only one side was possible, the one where the tree ended almost at the front door of the house.

"Here we go," I said, and bounced over the curb and drove with hope. As I passed between the tree and the front-door steps, the car scraped limbs on my side with a nauseating

47

grate, and on Leonard's side I heard one of the tires against the concrete steps; it made a sound like an electric can opener for a moment, then we were on the wider part of the yard and around the tree. I kept going, across the yard and off the curb and into the street, past the middle school, the yard of which was festooned with all manner of limbs and papers and even a tumbled-over car.

Damn, what a storm.

Back on the main street, I gave the car the gas, turned left when another pile of broken limbs and unidentifiable debris kept us from going forward. On down the narrow street I went. We sailed over a bridge with water running over it, and the water caught us and moved us to the right. The door on Leonard's side screamed as the concrete bridge gave it a body job, and then we were over the bridge and on the road, where there was less water.

To our right, a water park was now surely a water park. Floodwater had filled the pools and the whole place was a lake with metal tubing and metal platforms rising out of it. It reminded me of the skeletal ruins of a long-dead dinosaur.

Straight ahead was all we had as a way of escape. We drove by my dentist's office on the left, but I didn't honk, and continued with only the headlights to show us the way.

On we went, toward the loop, but when we got there, a left turn was out of the question. Cars were stacked there like tumbled dominoes. It looked as if they had been washed down from the parking lots of a housing division just above the loop. On the right, there were limbs and unidentifiable wads of debris. All routes were blocked except for a squeeze-through path on the right side of the road, around a turned-over tractor-trailer. It had most likely been trying to make the corner too fast in too much water.

We took that route, brushing up against the tractor-trailer, scraping some more paint off the left side of the car with a noise like fingernails on a chalkboard, and then we were around it.

I let out a satisfied sigh. Looked like smooth sailing for quite a way. Then the tire that had scraped concrete earlier blew out.

12

The car spun on the wet concrete and I tried to correct it with a gentle nudging of the brakes and a slight turn into the skid as Leonard said, "About par."

When I finally got the car to stop spinning, we were facing in the wrong direction, toward the overturned tractor-trailer. I popped the hatch, and me and Leonard got out, and set the wheelchair out and pulled up the back flooring to get to the spare and the jack. The tire was a temporary tire, because the car manufacturer was too special to put a real tire back there. It was small and thin, like a life preserver for a three-year-old. The jack was one of those kinds I hate. I missed the old sort where you just stuck it under a spot on the car, put on the emergency brake, jacked the car up, and changed the tire. Now you had to put a rod in a hole under the car and crank it. It was a little like a mastiff trying to get his dick into a Chihuahua. It took patience, something I was short on at that moment.

Leonard said, "I hate everybody and everything."

I eventually got it in position with a lot of cussing and encouragement from Leonard. I offered to let him do it, but he declined, twice. He seemed to think he was better in a coaching capacity.

The rain beat on us like galley-slave whips, but we got the tire off and changed, threw the jack, such as it was, into the back of the car, rolled the tire into the street, put the wheelchair in, and closed the hatch. Then we saw car lights sliding out onto the highway, moving toward the overturned tractor-trailer.

Through a gap in cab and trailer, we could see the white Lincoln. They had gotten out of the rut and past all the crap, and since there was only one way to go, they knew that's the way we had to have gone.

We jumped into the Prius, and I turned it around and drove hard as the car would go, that little tire making the car feel like it was limping on a short leg. I reached the end of the road. Billboards had been knocked down and laid into the street along with their metal racking, so I took a left, which was not a choice but the only path, as to the right there was a giant sycamore lying across the highway.

If something else fell into our path, we were pretty much boned.

We knew it wouldn't take the Lincoln long, with a little scraping, to get around the tractor-trailer, but it might take them a bit longer than it took us. The Prius was small and maneuverable, the Lincoln less so, but when it came to motor power, we were riding a bicycle and they were riding a jet.

As expected, in minutes, we saw the Lincoln's lights pop up behind us. They were far back, but soon they would close. We had the shotgun and the pistol I took from Big Guy, and there was the gun I had placed in the glove box, but I had a feeling they had a lot of heavy armament, and I had no idea how many were in the car. Was it just Big Guy and that creepy little fuck, or were there more? The Lincoln had room for quite a gathering.

"Hey, are there train tracks up here?" Leonard asked.

I knew there weren't but immediately understood why he had said that. I could hear what sounded like a train. I rolled the window down, heard that pathetic tire bumping uncomfortably over the road, and then I saw the trees to our left part, and out of that came a howling black wind and a wet whistle of rain—a twister, nature's freight train.

13

When I came to, the car was upside down.

In the rush not to have our heads blown off by our friends at the hospital, none of us had put on seat belts. I lay on the ceiling of the car with the girl lying over my chest. The IV had come out and something wet from the IV bag had run over me and made me feel sticky and cold. Leonard lay with his legs across mine. He wasn't moving.

It was light outside, but it was a muted light, and there was still rain, but not like before, and the wind was no longer howling. The tornado train had come and gone.

I gently got out from under the girl, trying not to put my hands on her naked ass—she was pretty exposed in that hospital gown—and then I eased over to Leonard.

"Goddamn," he said as I touched him.

"You hurting anywhere?"

"Question ought to be, where am I not hurting? But I think I'm okay. You?"

"Far as I can tell."

"The girl?"

"She's still breathing."

It was a chore but I got a door open even though the car was upside down. It grated in the mud, and then it hung, but I was able to squeeze out. That's when I noticed the back hatch had twisted off like it was made of wet cardboard. Would have been nicer had I noticed that right away. I was lucky I knew who I was.

Leonard and I got the girl out that way.

I found the shotgun and then the handgun, which I put in my pocket, and then we looked around carefully to see if our friends in the Lincoln were about. It was possible the tornado had missed them, and it was possible it had hit them too. It sure was one hell of a wind.

We tried our cell phones, as it was the first time we'd had a minute to consider it. I remembered my battery was dead, and Leonard didn't have any service, so we might as well have been carrying turnips.

"Now what?" Leonard said.

"We take turns toting her."

"Where to?"

"Good question."

I looked at the sky. It was a pearly mist and the mist was damp on our faces. There were no clouds, and though there was light, the sun wasn't visible. I was trembling a bit with the cold, and the girl certainly was.

"Feels and looks like the end of the world," I said.

Leonard helped boost the girl onto my shoulder, tried to pull the gown around her a little and tie it off. It wasn't perfect, but it gave her some modesty and made us feel better. Leonard carried the shotgun and crawled back inside the car and got the pistol from the glove box and put it in his belt.

I carried the girl along what served as a trail, though there was twisted wood everywhere, and we constantly had to navigate around or between debris.

The tornado had cut a path through the forest, and we followed that path, even though it was in places littered with tree limbs and pieces of tin and shingles that had been torn off houses or barns. We had no idea where we were going but had decided the highway might not be a good idea, as the Lincoln and its occupants might be up there. For all we knew, they might be making their way through the woods on foot, trying to find us.

I looked at my watch, realized we couldn't have been knocked out long. I had seen the time on the dashboard clock shortly before the tornado tossed the car around like a toy, and only about a half hour had passed. That made me think the thugs had experienced the storm as well, otherwise they would have found us easily enough. Didn't want to be tacky about it, but I hoped the tornado had wadded them and the Lincoln up and tossed them into the Gulf of Mexico.

After a long time walking, switching the girl out occasionally, we heard birds rise up in a great blast of wings, and then we saw that they were rising off a large misty patch of water, and then we generally knew where we were.

Lake LaBorde.

We looked out at it. It was impossibly swollen. It swelled shiny into the trees on the far side of the lake and washed up against the doors of lake houses over there that had once had frontage between themselves and the lake.

"I was sure we were going in the other direction," Leonard said. "I can't tell north from south under this sky."

"This means we aren't anywhere near help . . . wait. What's that?"

I could see a small cabin through the trees. It was always iffy these days to come up on someone unexpectedly, because now everyone had learned to live in fear from television news, and people who wanted to be sure they were safe might be packing enough guns for defense against an invasion from Mars. They might shoot on sight if they saw us come out of the woods, me with a girl slung over my shoulder like a hunter bringing home a deer.

She wasn't heavy, but she was heavy enough, and I was getting tired and was bone damp. I was chilled and hungry, and while whoever was in the cabin might shoot us, I was willing to chance it, since those in the Lincoln definitely would. Why they had cut the girl's tongue and come after her was still an unknown, but I was quite certain they were unpleasant people and now we too were on their shit list.

When we got to the cabin, I switched the girl to Leonard

and went up to the porch. There was still that whole thing about a black guy showing up on your porch unexpected, and we thought we'd put our best foot forward with a white foot.

I knocked on the door several times, but no one answered. I walked around the cabin, past an overturned barbecue grill and a little shed with a padlock on the door. The water from the lake had washed up around the shed, but the front of it was still clear.

I knocked on the back door of the cabin with the same lack of results, and then I walked around and looked in the windows. It looked dead inside, like no one had been there for a while. I got out my lock-pick kit, which is really a couple of little picks I have in my wallet, and worked on the back door and popped it open easy.

I went inside and looked around. I tried the light switch. Nope. Electricity was out over here too. Expected, but disappointing.

I ran my hand over a table. It was coated with dust. Same for the couch and the bar that separated the kitchen from the living room. It was a small two-story cabin. I went upstairs, calling out in case someone was asleep, but no one answered. Up there I found an open door that led into a bedroom. On the bed, under a blanket of flies, was a corpse. I couldn't tell if it was a man or woman, as the person had been dead some time. The corpse was dressed in pajamas, but they were the sort either a man or a woman might wear. The person's hair was short, but lots of women had short hair. A large revolver was near the withered, nearly skeletal hand, and what had been the person's head was broken open and some of what had been in it was in dark, dried wads on the wall. A window was open. Which was how the flies had got in.

I crept out and closed the door. I didn't know how long the person had been dead, but it seemed obvious they had got that way by their own hand and it had been long enough ago to allow a lot of flies to cluster.

I walked down the hall and came to glass double doors. They looked out onto a roofed deck surrounded by wooden rails. There was a heavy metal chair there, turned over and caught up in the railing. I didn't open the doors and go out there.

Downstairs, I opened the front door and signaled Leonard, who was standing in the misting rain with a frown on his face. He brought the girl in and laid her out on the couch, used couch pillows to prop up her head. There was a thin folded cover on the back of the couch, and he put that over her.

"She hasn't got the bag and the juice anymore," he said. "She needs a doctor."

"We'll just have to make her comfortable for now," I said. I told him what was upstairs.

"Well, shit. Aren't we on a run of luck?"

"Whoever is up there, their luck is worse."

"I'm sorry and everything, but my main problem right now is I'm starving," Leonard said.

The refrigerator was full of food, and the electricity hadn't been out so long as to allow things to rot. It was like it had been waiting on us.

Well, mostly. There was a gallon of milk that turned out to be spoiled, as it had been in there probably since the person upstairs decided to redecorate the wall. Electricity or no electricity, it had turned into a white glob of stink. I took it outside, found a big fifty-five-gallon drum for trash next to the overturned barbecue grill, and dropped it in. It was the only thing in the drum.

I was at a spot now where I could see behind the shed and through the twisted branches of a fallen sweet gum tree lying partially in the water. There was a long dock and a pretty good-size boat out there with a roof and fishing chairs fastened to a deck at the back. Of course, it was riding high in the water. So high it had lifted up over a weathered dock. The weight of it was starting to cause the dock to collapse. The boat surely belonged to the fly target upstairs.

I went back in the house. Leonard had found some TV dinners, but since the microwave didn't work, that wasn't all that much of a help. I found a set of a dozen keys on a ring hung on a nail by the door and went out to the little shed near the barbecue grill to try them.

After going through seven or eight keys, I found one that worked on the padlock. I opened the shed. Inside there were the usual things—a chain saw, general tools on a wall rack. A snakeskin on the floor. I knew the mice were in there because I could hear them squeaking. I prowled around in the shadows until I found a bag of charcoal and some flammable liquid in a squeeze bottle. I also found one of those things you could press and start a spark with. I tried it. It didn't work. I found a box of large kitchen matches. I shoved the matches into the windbreaker pocket that didn't house the gun.

The misting rain had ceased, so I felt I could get a fire going in the grill. I went over and righted it and put some charcoal in. I used the fluid in the squeeze bottle to coat it. I lit the doused charcoal directly with one of the kitchen matches. A flame jumped up and nearly took my eyebrows. I cocked the cooker lid over the fire without closing it all the way, then went back inside the cabin.

Leonard found a beer and a bottle of ginger ale in the fridge, and he pulled those out. I carried the TV dinners outside. They were enchiladas in paper containers, the kind designed for microwaves. I set them on the ground, went back inside, and me and Leonard looked through the shelves until I came across some aluminum foil.

Outside I shook the food out of the boxes and wrapped them in the foil and put them on the grill, waited impatiently while they heated up. I went inside and found some plates, went back out, put the food on those by nudging it loose from the foil with a stick, and took it all inside.

I sat the plates on the table. Leonard had found forks, and he gave me one, and we unrolled the foil and ate. It wasn't half-bad, though there were some cool spots in it. I had been too hungry to let them heat properly. I drank warm ginger ale and Leonard drank the warm beer.

I put the plates in the sink and washed them with tap water and bottled soap. I didn't want to leave the dead person a heap of dirty plates.

The wind began to whistle outside, and the rain picked up again, and the sky turned darker.

I said, "Damn it. Just quit already, will you?"

Leonard said, "I found some candles."

"Not sure we want to light them," I said. "The Lincoln folks may be searching for us."

"Good point."

Leonard went through the cabin, looking about. He went upstairs too, came down carrying a deer rifle and a box of ammunition. "We might need this."

"There's the handgun too," I said. "You know, next to the corpse."

"We'll let the dead keep it for now."

Leonard went over and sat by the window near the front door and pulled the curtain to, then pushed it slightly aside at one corner so he could see outside. He sat with the rifle in his lap. He put the box of ammunition in his windbreaker pocket.

I went around and pulled all the other curtains closed and locked the back door.

Then I checked on the girl. She was still out. I assumed that was due to the drugs she had been given, maybe what had been in the IV bag. She was breathing evenly.

In the bathroom, I found some over-the-counter pain relievers. I brought the bottle out with me, used a cutting board and the butt of a butcher knife to grind a few pills into a powder, and then I put the stuff in a cup, dampened it with water, let it set. I planned to give it to the girl if she woke up, so I thought it needed to be easy to take. I put the bottle of pills in my pocket.

I found a chair to sit in. There was a spare couch pillow. I got up and took it and put it behind my head. I wondered how many rounds were left in the pump shotgun. I wondered how many flies were on the corpse upstairs. Would we go to Mars in my lifetime? It was stuff like that running through my exhausted brain.

The chair I was in was a stuffed chair. It was comfortable. It was the most comfortable chair I had ever sat in since I was born. I yawned.

Leonard said, "Go to sleep, Hap. I got this."

He didn't have to tell me twice.

14

When I came awake, the wind was still blowing and the rain was still coming down. The sky was partially light, but the shadows were creeping in, dragging night along after them. I had slept a long time and I felt slightly refreshed.

I took Leonard's spot and the rifle, and Leonard took my chair. He was asleep immediately.

I'm not sure how long I sat there looking out the window, but at one point I chose to go upstairs to the deck, as I thought it might be a better vantage point. I opened the glass doors and stepped out. The rain was blowing onto the deck and splattering at my feet and hammering on the roof above. I stayed back enough to not get wet, close to the door. It was then that I saw something moving in the tangled woods beyond. And then I didn't see it anymore. I stepped back through the open doors and stood there, just inside.

It was starting to be solid dark again, and as the night oozed in with its wind and its rain, it was harder to see. I stood there for several long minutes watching that spot, but I didn't see anything again, and now it was so dark if a bear were dancing in a top hat, I couldn't have seen him. Though I would have liked to.

And then lightning cut across the sky and cracked a tree in the woods, and in that flash, I saw Big Guy and, off to his right, what I think was a woman. Pale-skinned with a rain hood around her head, damp black hair dangling out from under it, plastered wet against her cheeks.

Both wore black and they both had very nasty-looking guns. I couldn't tell what kind, but I was pretty sure they weren't water guns.

When the lightning was gone, they were out of sight, so I went downstairs quickly and shook Leonard awake.

"They've found us," I said.

He got up and got the shotgun I had been carrying. The handguns were still on us.

"I guess we play Alamo," he said.

"I don't want to. Hey, the boat out back."

I didn't have to say it twice. Leonard gave me the shotgun, picked the girl up off the couch, and carried her in his arms like a baby. She made a moaning sound. They headed out the back door, and I followed.

I thought, All right, they may assume we're here, but they don't know that for sure.

Or maybe they did. Maybe one of them or all of them were trackers. Maybe they had a pack of bloodhounds with them.

One thing I'd say for them—storm, tornado, what have you, they were not quitters.

Outside we moved swiftly toward the boat. We had to climb over a tree trunk and push through some shattered limbs with wet leaves on them, but we made it to the sagging dock and finally onto the boat.

Leonard tossed loose the tie lines that held the boat to the dock. It was a tenuous connection. A little bit more storm, and the dock wouldn't be there to hold anything.

We pushed against the boat, and it came off the dock with a scraping sound that made me turn and look back at the cabin.

No one yet.

I kept my guard position there on the deck, giving Leonard time to get the girl inside. No one shot at me. No flashlights bobbed our way.

I had the ring of keys in my pocket and hoped like hell one of them was for the boat. I ended my vigil and went into the wheelhouse. There was a short stairway that led down, and I logically assumed that's where the girl was, that Leonard had tucked her away down there. She had certainly been through hell, although she'd spent most of it asleep.

I fumbled with the key ring while Leonard came up from below and stood at one of the wheelhouse windows and looked out. The view wasn't a good one, as there was a tree or two in the way, mainly that big sweet gum, plus the shed. From where we were, we could see in the direction of the back door, but the night had pretty much swallowed it and the cabin.

I found a key that fit. I hoped there was gas in the engine and the damn craft was in working condition.

I said, "I'm going to try and start it."

"Wait," Leonard said. He put the shotgun aside and picked up the rifle I had leaned against a wall.

He gently opened the door to the cabin, stepped on deck. I started the engine. It hummed like a champ. I heard a shot, and something struck the boat, and then a lot of shots struck the boat. I heard Leonard open up with the rifle, less rapid-fire, but by then I was steering us away from the dock and pushing out into the lake.

Bullets snapped. The boat pinged and ripped in places I hoped weren't serious. Lightning flashed across the water, and the wind made the water swell and the night was as solid as a big black brick.

I didn't try to turn on any lights. I gave the boat the throttle and went on into darkness, hoping there wasn't anything I might hit.

15

When Leonard came into the wheelhouse, I said, "You okay?"

"Fine."

"Hit anything?"

"I shot at the gunfire. I don't know. The boat took some shots, though. Guess it's okay."

"We aren't sinking," I said. "Better check on the girl."

Leonard went down, came back in a short time.

"She's all right. Still out but starting to stir some. Did you notice she smells like strawberries?"

"I did."

"Shampoo, I guess."

I reached in my pocket and took out the pills I had taken from the cabin. "Doubt she can swallow these," I said. "Mashed her up a batch at the cabin but never got around to giving it to her. If you can find a cup and a spoon down there, if there's water, maybe you can crush them up, make a liquid. You might give them to her if she wakes up."

"Right now, all I'm worried about is this black water. I can crush pills anytime."

I fumbled around until I found the lights, and when I hit them, the water lit up, and so did the wheelhouse.

"I think we're far enough away now," I said.

"Man, they are relentless."

"Won't be the first time we've dealt with their sort," I said.

"It'll be the first time we're as old and tired as we are. And you know what? I think it may be the first time we've dealt with their sort. They are major prepared."

The lake was littered with floating trees and all manner of windblown and rain-pushed debris. The boat rode rough and I wasn't particularly skilled at driving it. A raccoon could have been trained to do better than I was doing, though it would have to be a smart raccoon.

I could sometimes see cabins on shore, when my lights caught them or the lightning revealed them. They were all dark and lifeless.

The lake was large, larger now due to all the storm waters, and I decided to push across it, try and find a place to dock, see if we could get help. Leonard tried his phone again, but no dice. He figured a tower was blown down.

I thought of Brett and Chance and Reba, and I hoped they were okay. Was the house still standing? Was Buffy the Biscuit Slayer under the bed?

I wished I were under the bed.

On through the rainy night and over the leaping water we went, and soon we were on the far side of the lake. In the lights from our boat I could see the water had risen far above the shoreline, and I feared there were hidden docks under it, so I tried to ease in, pulling back on the throttle. It was a good thing I did, because we bumped up against something that gave the boat a jolt.

Leonard went outside and leaned over the railing with a flashlight that he'd found in the wheelhouse. He came back inside, said, "There's limbs everywhere, and I mean big limbs. There's no way you're going to slide it in here."

I backed the boat off and gradually swung it around, and with my lack of experience it wasn't any harder than trying to turn a dead whale.

Back on the open water, we went along for a while, and finally the rain ceased, and the sky lightened some, and after a while we could see a star or two peeking through strips of dark rain-packed clouds. Then I saw lights suddenly pop on along the shoreline. Houses were visible now. The lights made them look warm. The electric company had been hard at work.

I eased toward the shoreline there and found a place I could run the boat aground. I throttled it up big-time and shot it forward. It bounced on the water like the lake was made of hard concrete. The boat went onto the shore even as I throttled it back; it was too late to make a comfortable nose-in landing, and the bumping water helped jump us onto a patch of mud. The bumping was hard enough to knock Leonard down and hard enough to make my teeth bang together and nearly cause my knee to go out from under me.

I killed the engine, and we went down and turned on the cabin light, found our girl still sleeping, quite comfortably. She hadn't even been shaken out of the bed.

Leonard went through the little closet down there, found a pair of men's pants and a rain poncho.

"You remember all I did was put pants on her," Leonard said.

"Gotcha."

"You can turn your head, Hap."

"I was going to. What about you?"

"I'm gay and I'm putting the pants on. I don't get excited by naked women. I want to double note that."

I turned my back as Leonard worked her pants on and pulled the yellow rain poncho over her head. I turned around again as she groaned and her eyes opened.

She started fighting immediately but then must have realized who Leonard was, remembered he had thrown her in the back of the car in the first place. She looked over at me. I could see her swole tongue. It looked like there was a pale, stuffed sock in her mouth. She tried to talk, but her words were like cars trying to get around a too-narrow pass in the mountains. They tumbled off into sounds that meant nothing.

"Take it easy," I said.

"You can zip yourself up," Leonard said. "Whoever those

pants belong to was a lot bigger than you, but it beats traveling around with your butt hanging out."

It was then that she realized she had been wearing nothing but a hospital gown. She reached under the poncho and clutched at it, gave me a confused look.

"You were in the hospital," I said. "Some folks came for you. Not nice folks. They wanted to shoot you."

"And us, I might add," Leonard said.

"Are you in pain?" I said.

She shook her head gently.

"I have some over-the-counter pain stuff. I can mash it up and maybe you could drink it."

She shook her head again.

"All right, so next thing we do is get the hell out of here."

16

Considering people were trying to kill us, we hesitated to leave the shotgun and the rifle, but finally decided we had lost our pursuers, at least for now, and the best thing for us to do was to head out and make for the highway. It had to be out there somewhere.

We kept the handguns, tucked them under our wet shirts. We left the boat and started hiking out, the girl walking now but doing a weak job of it. Still, it beat carrying her.

We didn't stop by houses and ask for help. It had been a long time since you could knock on someone's door and ask for assistance and get it. No one trusted anyone these days.

There was a trail from the lake between two cabins, and we took that. Some dogs barked at us. I glanced down the shoreline and saw more lights coming on in lakefront homes.

We followed the trail to a little road that was an exit for

those who lived along the lake. In short time we began to hear a buzzing sound, and then the sound grew louder. We came out on the edge of the highway. There were trucks there, people working, lots of lights. The electric company restoring power.

I went over and talked to one of the workers, a little Hispanic guy with a yellow hard hat. Others came over to see what we were about. They gave us some water, which even the girl managed to drink around her fat tongue. Then they called the cops for us over their radio. Before too long, perhaps an hour, a car came out and parked near the truck we were leaning on, the girl sitting inside of it.

The driver's door of the car opened and someone got out.

It was Manny.

17

We were dry and warm and had coffee and sandwiches that a short, stout cop named Alton had bought for us. He brought the sandwiches in a couple of bags and stood around, holding a white bakery box under his arm. He smiled at us.

Leonard and I ate and felt better, but the girl couldn't eat, not with that tongue. She did get some dry clothes, though, something Manny rustled up. Manny got a nurse over to the police station, thinking the hospital might still be unsafe, and a jail cell with an open door and a soft bunk became the girl's hangout.

The girl had got some fluids in her, thanks to the nurse, and now she was asleep again with an IV hooked up to her. We knew nothing more than we had when we first found her on the road, except some people wanted her tortured and dead. Right now, they didn't like me and Leonard too much either, but my guess was they had no idea who we were. Just a couple of meddlers.

"I think we'll keep her here for a bit," Manny said. "She seems stable enough. Then we have to consider if we'll send her back to the hospital with more cops to watch her. We have your descriptions of the shooters you saw, and that helps."

"These guys," Leonard said, "they strike me as professional, maybe ex-military. One of them, he's like a kung fu rabbit. Me and Hap, we're trained, we're pretty good, but this guy is crazy good and acrobatic. Not that big a guy either, but he didn't mind coming after both of us at the same time."

"And he damn near beat us," I said.

"I don't know about that," Leonard said.

"Thing is," Manny said, "he doesn't know who either of you are. That's to your advantage."

"What I was thinking," I said. "But we don't actually know how many of them there are and who they are connected to."

Alton was standing in the doorway, a shoulder against the door frame. He watched us talk and eat, still with the white box under his arm. He had one of those sad faces, like a hound dog with a stomach ailment.

"For them, we were in the wrong place at the wrong time," I said. "They weren't taking names. Damn. What about the lady at the hospital? She make it?"

Manny shook her head. "Neither she nor the officer survived."

"Guys did the shootings were sure of themselves. Me and Leonard, we had a streak of luck."

"Bad luck," Leonard said.

"Neither of you are dead," Manny said. "There's some good luck in there someplace."

"You have a point," Leonard said.

"Here's what I think," she said. "Since they don't know who you are, you're out of this. You can go home and put your feet up. My guess is the only person they really want is her. You were just in the way. When she wakes up, I'm going to get her a writing pad, ask some questions."

"I could use some rest," I said.

"Me too," Leonard said.

"You got a lot more explaining to do," Manny said. "Breaking into a cabin, stealing a boat. Taking the girl from the hospital. But it's all logical survival stuff."

"What about whoever was dead in that cabin?" I said.

"We're looking into it. And by the way, I am the acting chief until Hanson gets back from his trip. It was decided last night."

"A little promotion," I said.

"Temporary," she said.

"What time is it?" I said.

Manny hesitated. She wasn't sure. She looked at Alton.

"Late morning," Alton said.

We had been in there since before daybreak, telling Manny all that had happened, all that we'd seen.

"I'm hitting the bricks again," Alton said. "At least where I can still see bricks, concrete. Lot of water out there. I got to put this up first." Alton lifted the box under his arm to show us what he was putting away, stepped out and went down the hall.

"Alton's all right," Manny said. "He's new, comes from a little cop shop somewhere in Louisiana, I think. Don't remember exactly. Transferred here a few months back. He'll do fine."

"Glad to hear it," I said.

"Poor guy, got a sick kid, and I don't mean with the flu. Really sick, some kind of neurological disease. Costs a lot to take care of his daughter, Ginger's her name, I think. He has another job being a part-time rent-a-cop, and his wife works two jobs, one as a baker. She's the one bakes the pies he brings in. That's what's in the box. His rule is whoever wants some can have it, as long as he gets a slice."

"Maybe it's a leftover from work," Leonard said.

Manny frowned at Leonard. "Whatever, he brings them in. But that poor kid, that poor family, even with insurance and additional government aid, and there's less of that all the time, they can hardly make ends meet. Actually, I doubt they do meet." She shook her head. "I think about having kids once in a while, but then I wonder if I have some genetic mess lurking inside me that will cause a kid to not be right, or the father has it, or we both have it. I don't even date much these days. Well, Cason, who you know, but we mainly just shag and we're both heavy on the protection. He likes to wear handcuffs and do it with a doughnut in his mouth."

"I don't want to hear about it," I said.

"Wait," Leonard said. "A doughnut?"

"No, I was just trying to make Hap uncomfortable."

"Shit, he likes doughnuts," Leonard said.

Manny grinned. "Well, our relationship may not be about doughnuts, but like that old Haggard song, 'It's Not Love, But It's Not Bad.'"

Since we no longer had a car and neither of us had a working phone, I used the office landline to call Brett and ask her to pick us up. Right then there wasn't anything I wanted more than being home in a nice dry and warm place that didn't have cops in it.

We stood outside the cop shop waiting for her to show up. There was a thin veneer of water over everything. We had learned from Manny that the outskirts of the town, the low places, were now deep water. We watched as Alton drove his cop car around the building, onto a side street.

On the far side of the street, there was a swollen creek, and water had run out of it and was splashing over the curb. Some of the water was running down a drain near where the road met the highway. It was a lot of water, and that drain could hold only so much.

When Brett arrived, we climbed in the car, and she turned in the seat and checked us out.

She wrinkled her brow, said, "You boys really shouldn't ever go outside. It always turns bad."

18

When Leonard and I walked in, Buffy the Dog licked our faces and wagged her tail. Chance peppered us with questions, while Reba sat in a chair at the table where we were gathered and watched us like we were monkeys in a zoo. She was a twelve-year-old child, and she seemed way too wise and just a little evil. Leonard nearly always called her the Four-Hundred-Year-Old Vampire.

After we told of our adventures, Reba said, "Y'all could have got yourself shot. And for some whitey."

"I'm a whitey," I said.

"Another whitey, standing right here," Brett said.

"Make that three," Chance said.

"I'm not in the club," Leonard said.

"Yeah," Reba said. "All y'all white except Leonard, and he's just an asshole, but you said she was real white."

"Albinism," I said.

"She got them pink eyes?"

"Light eyes," I said. "Not pink."

"I thought they had pink eyes, like a rabbit or some such."

"Albinism varies, Reba," I said. "She's a very pretty girl, or young woman. Frankly, she's so small and young-looking, it's hard to tell. She might be eighteen, she might be thirty."

"That's cause she's a Chinaman," Reba said. "They look young when they're a hundred years old."

"You can take the girl out of the projects," Leonard said, "but you can't take the projects out of the girl."

"You talking big, country man," she said. "Listening to all that cracker music and shit. You ought to put some shine on your black ass."

Leonard gave her a look that could have made a bear call a taxi. "And you ought to shut up before I set you on fire, you little shit."

"Come on, Leonard," Chance said. "She's a kid. Talk nice."

"Naw," Reba said, and she might have been the bear's taxi driver. "Bring it, cowboy."

I saw Leonard fume and perhaps consider how long he would be in prison for killing a child. "Last time I rescue your ass," Leonard said.

"Yeah, well, you get killed, you ain't rescuing no one's ass," she said, and I thought I detected a small catch in her voice.

Leonard relaxed. "No way. Me and Hap, we're invincible."

"No, we're not," I said.

"Well, we're tough," Leonard said.

"Ain't nobody tough enough in the end," Reba said.

Chance got up and came over and put her arm around Reba. "They're both fine."

"Hell, I don't care," Reba said. She didn't look at either of us when she said it.

"I know what," Brett said. "How about I fix some lunch? You boys want coffee?"

"That would be good," I said.

"Good," she said. "I'll order us a couple of pizzas. Hap, start the coffee."

"That's not fixing lunch," I said.

"It's my way of fixing lunch," she said.

19

A couple days passed, and the weather stayed volatile. Every time it cleared up and looked as if it was going to stabilize, a black cloud would appear in the distance and the rain and the wind would come again and howl loud enough to scare the shit out of a lion.

The Atlantic kept brewing up unseasonable tropical storms, and it was said a hurricane about the size of Rhode Island was going to make landfall in Houston. It might even make it to LaBorde.

The news told us not to take it lightly, to prepare and expect storm damage. It warned that though it was rare for a hurricane to make its way this far inland, this one looked highly possible, and maybe with category 3 winds. The weather lady suggested we stock up on food, flashlight batteries, and candles.

We had already lost one window on the house due to flying debris, and I expected it would be worse in a few days. I nailed some plywood over the missing window. When the weather settled down, I planned to replace it.

Brett Sawyer Investigations was out of work right then. No one needed a cheating spouse followed, so we were mostly sitting around. Pookie was still away, so Leonard had been staying with us.

It was a crowded house. Chance and Reba gave up the bedroom, where Chance had slept in the bed and Reba on an air mattress. Leonard took their place in there. Chance ended up on the couch, and Reba had the air mattress on the floor next to it. Buffy slept with Reba. Reba loved that dog and cuddled her like she was a big stuffed toy. It seemed as if Buffy was pretending to be one.

Something about the storms, and the big one that might be coming, caused me to give my life a lot of consideration. The storms were out of season that year, and so was I. Leonard and I joked, but I was beginning to feel my age.

I used to heal practically overnight, but now my bones ached from past encounters, and I found I enjoyed lying about more, staying near Brett. We filled in places that the other lacked, and no doubt, I got the better end of that deal.

We had recently married after living together for years. There had been a couple of separations, a worry here and there about things the three of us had done in the name of justice, as if we had any right to deal out justice. But we had anyway. Leonard and Brett were fine with that. They slept well at night. They were pragmatic. Me, I was a wounded idealist with a liberal limp. I wanted justice, but I wanted hope, and I wanted to be the old me, the person I was before I had taken a life.

I was not a pacifist, but I didn't want to keep trying to solve problems with weapons and fists. The guilt of that had begun to outweigh the satisfaction.

Maybe it was time me and Leonard pulled out a couple of rocking chairs. We could just peek through windows to see who was cheating on who and cash our checks, take it easy.

We couldn't set everything right. Hell, me and Leonard had done all we could for that girl, and now the cops had her and she was safe. We were done.

Sure. It was over.

Like hell it was.

20

One morning I got the call from Manny.

"Here's what we've learned. The girl is feeling much better. She wrote down her name. It's Nikki. She won't say her last name. We've asked her what happened, what's going on? She wrote that she wanted you and Leonard. Actually, she wrote, 'I want the black guy and the white guy who saved me.'"

"Okay."

"She's still here at the station. Doesn't want to go to the hospital. I don't blame her. In a nest of cops is probably the safest place she could be. Her tongue swelling has gone down. She might even be able to talk in a few days, and if she is, will you two come down and hear what she has to say so we can hear it too? Or maybe she writes it all down for you. Doesn't matter. But I'd like for you to come."

"We can do that," I said.

"Should you ask Leonard?"

"I know what his answer will be. We've been talking about her, wondering how she was, what had happened to her. Wondering if someone out there was still determined to kill her."

"Wondering the same myself. I'll call you when I think she's ready for it, because right now she's on some strong pain relievers and sleeps a lot. Outside of her tongue cut like that, almost cut off, she's all right. Looks like the doctor stitched it back together. The doctor, she says Nikki will be fine in time. But I wanted to know you two can be here so I could tell her. Have you heard the weather report?"

"I quit listening. It's always bad."

"It's going to get worse. A series of tornadoes are expected for our area. Lots of rain and high wind the rest of the time, and then we'll get some hurricane from the Gulf. Probably fire and pestilence to follow, could be a plague of boils and locusts, maybe an egg and bacon shortage to top things off."

"Thanks for making my day."

"Hey, blame global warming, not me. Who the hell expects hurricanes this time of year. Mother Earth hates us."

•   •   •

That night I came down from the bedroom, where I had been reading in bed beside Brett, and found Leonard in the kitchen with Reba. There was a bag of vanilla cookies on the table and she had a glass of milk and he had a large cup of coffee. I could smell the coffee when I came into the kitchen, and now I wanted some. I went over and put a decaf pod in the machine, put the cup under, and got that going.

"Now I get a cookie," Reba said.

"Just one," Leonard said.

Reba took one from the bag, dipped it in her milk like she was drowning someone she didn't like.

I sat at the table with them and told Leonard what Manny said.

"That little white girl ain't something oughta be messed with," Reba said. "White people get you killed. Real white one like that, she's nothing but trouble. More white on they ass, more trouble they is."

"You don't even know her," I said.

"Got some idea."

"I'm white."

"Done said that. And you trouble too. But guess you my trouble, and she ain't. She ain't oughta be none of yours."

Reba had seen some death in her young years, had been disappointed by people more than once. I couldn't blame her youthful cynicism, but sometimes, the depth of it for a child, the knowledge she had, pained me.

"She's got no one else right now," I said. "You know how that is."

Reba eyed me for a long moment, then looked at the sack

of cookies. "Ain't you supposed to take a turn?" she said to Leonard.

Leonard reached in the bag and took one. Reba turned the bag and took one for herself. "Now we even," she said.

"You're one ahead," Leonard said.

"Ain't I always?" she said.

21

Upstairs, back in bed with Brett, I told her what was going on, said, "You know what?"

"What," she said.

"I think you should take the girls, including the dog girl, and you should go someplace else for a while."

"Sending us out for our own protection again," she said. "I can take care of myself."

"I know that, but I'm not so sure about Chance and Reba or Buffy the Dog."

"I think you're being all macho, the man taking care of his little woman. You know what?"

"What?"

"I like that. I'm all for being an empowered female badass, but I still need someone to lift heavy things off the top closet shelf."

"There's nothing heavy up there."

"Now you're going to get technical. Listen, Hap, I do appreciate you watching out for me. But I can take care of myself, boy. I like the thought, but I've been known to be trouble myself."

"This is true."

"You're not the only one has murder in his history. You, me, and Leonard."

"Thing is, why have more? It's a heavy weight, and more just makes it heavier."

"And no one hates carrying it more than you."

"So you're really fine with what you've done? What we've done? Hell, what me and Leonard have done?"

"It's not about being fine with it, dear. It's about knowing why it was done. I never lie down and think I'm a random killer or that I did anything for money or profit."

"In my case, revenge has been in the soup a few times."

"But there was more to it than being angry about being cut off in traffic or someone beating you to a Walmart Black Friday sale. It was more complicated than just getting even. You've stepped on some bugs, Hap. Me and you and Leonard."

"We do a lot of stepping."

"When the law does its job, we don't need to do a thing. They don't always. And as you've said, when the law breaks the law or refuses to do its job, there is no law."

"I think I stole that from the *Billy Jack* movie. I don't know how much I believe it."

"I'm not saying it's cut and dried, but you really seem worried. More than usual. What exactly are you afraid of?"

"I'm not sure. The weather, for one. It's becoming worse, and if the weather reports hold, it's going to make LaBorde very wet."

"It's East Texas, baby. We always have storms."

"And there's those guys I told you about. They're bad news. They know what they're doing, and what they're doing is dangerous and ugly, and they are persistent. I've got an uncomfortable feeling about that girl, like maybe whatever went on with her is still going on, and me and Leonard are somehow in the pile. That leads to you guys."

"You said they don't know who you are."

"Things can be found out. Guys that have the kind of organization and weapons and determination these people do, well, they got money behind them. And if you got money, you have power, and you have connections. We can be found out, and then you're found out. All that leads to Chance and Reba. I need them taken care of, and you're the one to do it. They love you, they trust you, and as you said, you're a badass."

"Where would we go?"

"First time in our life, we got a little money," I said. "My life, anyway. Why not take advantage of it? We aren't going to be getting any private-investigation business in this weather, and me and Leonard will be tied up a little with Manny and the girl, so, you know, you could go most anyplace."

"And what if you go in to talk with Manny, and you're back in two hours?"

"Then I'll meet up with you guys."

Brett twisted her mouth the way she does when she's considering an idea.

"We could go to Tyler," she said. "I'd like to do some shopping. They got a Half Price Books there, a Thai place. I ate there when I bought Reba shoes. I like shoes too."

"All the shoes you got, it's like you got a lot more feet than two. It's like you're a centipede."

"They have a new theater there too. Lots of movies."

"That sounds good."

"They have a hotel right there in the mall. All kinds of stores. It's big-time for East Texas."

"Does the hotel allow dogs?"

"I don't know. Maybe not. If they don't, then the closest hotel to the mall that does allow dogs would be our pick."

"Sounding better and better."

"I'll be spending some serious money if I go over there."

"It's your money more than mine. I work for you, remember?"

"I never forget."

"So?"

"I'll give it some thought. We might do that. I do, you join us there when you're finished."

"Good. Go there and wait until you hear from me, stay as long as you need to stay. I'll catch up with you."

"Hap, you sound like you're really worried, not like you're excited about a vacation."

"I said as much."

"Yeah, but this feels different."

"That's because I'm really worried, but I'm not exactly sure what I'm worried about, and that worries me even more. I hope you'll take that vacation, and before it gets really stormy."

Brett rolled over and put her arm across my chest.

"Maybe we should see if we can make a storm ourselves."

"I'm feeling a bit like a tornado," I said.

"And I know a tornado alley you might like to visit."

"Oh my, girl, you are nasty."

"Uh-huh, I am."

22

————

 Time passed but the wind and rain didn't. The tornadoes
Manny warned me about came, but we were lucky and our
place wasn't hit by any. The twisters tore up the woods on
the eastern edge of town and took a few houses and mobile
homes out in the country on a sightseeing tour, and though
there were some minor injuries, no one was killed, though
there were reports of missing chickens.

That was a good thing, no one being hurt, though who
knows about the chickens. The morning Manny called us to
come down to the station, the weather was still bad. The sky
was black, the wind was high, and the rain was furious.

We drove to the cop shop in Leonard's truck, and as we
went, we saw the roofs of some houses were missing, and
there were plenty of shingles lying about like dead soldiers.
The streets were littered with wet leaves and paper. Now

and again, something unidentifiable blew by or against the truck.

Even that early in the day we drove with the lights on. There were few cars out, probably folks like us, doing only what they had to do. We reached the center of town. Leonard drove slow and easy because the brick streets were slick as owl shit. There were a couple cars crashed alongside the road. I wondered how long they had been there.

Stores were closed, even the café on the corner. We had to turn a street early because we could see parked city electric company trucks and workers wearing yellow slickers in our path.

It felt so eerie.

We took Pecan Street next to the bookstore, went up a ways, turned left, crossed North Street, and came to the rear of the cop shop.

There was a parking lot back there, and there were two police cars in the lot. One of them had a crumpled front end, most likely a result of the stormy weather. There was a white transport bus there too. It had wire mesh on the windows. It was an old bus and had once been used to transport prisoners, and from time to time it still was. According to Marvin, it was supposed to be sold in the next county auction.

We cruised through the back lot, went around the side of the building, and parked out front. There were only a couple of cars there.

We got out wearing our black hooded rain slickers ("Same alike," Reba called them) and made our way into the station, leaning into the wind the way you would if you were trying to push a truck uphill and feared a hernia.

The receptionist knew us and we walked over to the plasti-glass she was behind and spoke into the little grate that allowed our voices through but not much else. That glass, Marvin once said, was built like the Great Wall of China. Evelyn was always friendly and kept her kids' and grandkids' photos in frames on her desk, which bent like a horseshoe around her in what was a good-size room. She looked like a lady who loved bacon and grease. She wore big flowery explosions of cloth and always had a tall Styrofoam cup of something on her desk. She had hair like a wasps' nest, but it wasn't by accident—she styled it that way. There was enough hairspray on it to pin a wrestler to the mat, and she wore a flakey white lipstick that reminded me of cake frosting.

"How's things with the family?" Leonard said.

"Fine. You boys in new trouble yet?"

"Why, Evelyn," I said. "We don't get in trouble, we get in adventures."

"Is that what you call them?"

"Yeah," I said. "We go with that."

"That's not what Chief Hanson calls them," she said, and pointed at the door to the side of her office and buzzed the lock. With waves to her, we pushed the door and went in.

Manny was easy to find. She was in Hanson's office going over some paperwork. The door was open. We went in.

"Caught you working," I said.

"Pretending to work," she said.

"So how is she?" Leonard said, and we both took off our slickers and hung them on hooks on the back of the open door and sat.

"She can talk a little, but not for long. She gets tired and her tongue starts to hurt. She might talk some and write some. But she can communicate and claims she'll tell more with you guys here. I'm not sure what the attraction is."

"Sterling manhood," Leonard said. "There's nothing like a real man that's queer as a duck in trousers to bring out the enthusiasm of either sex."

"What about me?" I said. "I'm not gay."

"That sort of sets you back a notch," Leonard said. "But you'll do."

"That's funny," Manny said. "Just not enough."

"I think I'm perfectly manly," I said.

Leonard grinned at me. Manny chose not to get involved.

Manny got up and led us out of the office and down the hall. There was a jail cell at the back with its door swung wide, and Nikki was sitting up in a hospital bed that had been rolled in for her. She had a stack of pillows behind her head and at her back. She wore an orange jumpsuit, same as a criminal. She had an IV in her arm, and the bag for it hung on an IV rack. The nurse, a slim, older woman, nodded at us and then, without a word, got up and went out.

I guess Manny had her trained.

There were three chairs in the cell, and they had provided Nikki with a small table. There were four books on it, popular bestsellers. There was a yellow legal pad and a ballpoint pen beside them.

We sat in the chairs.

I smiled at Nikki. "How are you?"

"Terrible," she said. I understood her clearly, but there was an oddness about her voice. She had to pronounce the word "terrible" with painful care, and it arrived as if by banana boat.

"Looks like you got a lot of reading material," I said.

"Nurse's stuff," she said. "She's very sweet."

"Manny said you'd like to talk to us."

She nodded. She waved her hand, indicating we should come closer. We scooted our chairs nearer to the bed. When we were settled, Nikki reached out and took Leonard's hand and pulled it up on the little table and held it. It was quite a contrast, the hand of a snow-white woman grasping a hand as black as the bottom of a coal mine.

She took a deep breath, let it out, said, "I'm scared."

"We know what you're scared of," I said. "But we don't know who they are or why they're after you. That something you can explain?"

"Nicole Beckman."

The three of us just stared at her. She might as well have pulled a name out of a hat, stuck her finger on a name in the phone book, or said that Santa Claus had sent his elves after her.

"Who's that?" Manny said.

"A year ago," Nikki said, "she was murdered in her home, and her girlfriend was there with her."

I thought I had the answer. I said, "Are you the girlfriend?"

She shook her head gently. "I bat for the other team."

"Okay," I said. "How are you connected to her?"

"I'm not. Not really."

"Shit," Manny said. "Beckman. Yeah. Wait. I heard about that. Around Tyler, right?"

Nikki nodded.

Manny explained. "No one could figure out why Nicole Beckman was killed. No record. No indication of criminal activity of any kind. Someone broke in her house and blew her brains out while she was in bed. Her girlfriend was with her, and the girlfriend said the man with the gun came in and said to Nicole, 'Is your name Nicole Beckman?' She said it was, and he shot her, hit the girlfriend in the head with the stock of the shotgun, and got out of there quick. No one has any idea who it was killed Beckman, or why. Killer wore a mask, animal mask of some sort. The girlfriend said he seemed unsteady on his feet, like maybe he'd spent too much time at a bar. Odd observation, but I remember that's what she said, what was reported, anyway."

I was more baffled now than before I came to the station.

Leonard's mouth fell open, and I saw a look in his eye like a chicken that had just laid an egg and was mighty proud of it. He leaned forward in his chair, said, "And is Nikki short for something else?"

"Nicole," she said.

"And your last name is?" he said.

"Beckman."

23

Someone killed the wrong Nicole Beckman," Leonard said. "They were after you."

Nikki nodded.

She started talking, and although she eventually had to resort to writing it down, we got the complete story, and it was an odd one.

It boiled down to this, at least at first. The center of Nikki's problem was Larry Keith, aka One Mean Asshole.

When Nikki said that name, Manny knew who it was immediately, sketched in some background for us so as to save Nikki's tongue too much of a workout.

Larry operated a garage outside of Tyler, near Bullard, but he used it as a chop shop as well. Fix a car by day, chop one by night. Legitimate when the sun was up, crooked when the sun went down.

Larry was the son of Wilson Keith. We had heard of him. He was big in the Dixie Mafia. Leonard and I had put our hands into that dirt a few times and happily toppled some of those assholes off their thrones, but it was like whack-a-mole—someone new popped right up. Wilson Keith was that someone new, a former second or third in command that took over things due to design and attrition. Always suspected of this or that, always written about in the papers, mentioned on TV, but never caught with his hand in the cookie jar. He was as smooth as owl shit and twice as stinky.

Wilson set his son Larry up in business, and business was good. Larry was fond of older muscle cars when he could get them. Couldn't sell the whole car, he sold the parts. But no matter how hard the local law or the feds tried to nail him, they couldn't do it. It wasn't that Larry was all that smart, but his old man was. And as long as Larry followed the old man's lead, he stayed in the clear. He and his crew could take a car apart in seconds, redo it, and have it on a truck going up north about the time you pulled your coat on. They sold them way under the cost of the original cars. Theft has a low overhead.

Nikki said Larry's favorite car thief was a fellow named Pretty Boy Florence. He was a real pro, had been known to steal a car midday right off a car lot. He was quick, self-assured, and could talk a nun out of her underpants and convince her to buy them back. He had a girlfriend named Nicole Beckman. She knew all about what was going on. She was deeply in love with Pretty Boy, no matter that he was a thief.

That Nicole was our snow-white Nikki.

Nikki started talking again. Manny said, "If you're going to tell your story, I want the nurse here. I want to make sure we don't push you too hard or you don't overdo."

Manny got up and called the nurse in and I got up and went out and got another chair and brought it back. The nurse sat close to Nikki, but Nikki didn't let go of Leonard's hand.

Manny said to the nurse, "We want to make sure we aren't pushing her too hard and that she's not pushing herself too hard, but anything you hear tonight, it's confidential. You understand?"

"I understand," said the nurse. "And I appreciate being with my patient. I'm here for her health. You do what you got to do, and it's safe with me."

"Good," Manny said.

Nikki began talking again.

"One night I was out with Pretty Boy, and we were coming back from dinner, and he was always fun, so funny, and maybe at the bottom of it all, he wasn't that smart, but he dressed sharp and took me to nice places, and there was part of me that knew I was being shallow, that this guy was going nowhere fast and dragging me with him. But I loved him. I did. I dreaded the moments I was without him, but when I was with him I was, in the back of my mind, always wondering how I might shed myself of him. He was like having a dangerous wild animal for a pet, one that thinks you're the pet, and you know in your bones that pet isn't loyal, and one day it's going to turn and bite you, but, man, is it fluffy and cute, and there are such fine moments when you're with it.

"But this night, that was the night I had been dreading, that down-in-the-bones feel that something bad was coming. I can't tell you how many times I told myself I was standing on a railroad track and the train was heading for me and I ought to step off because the engineer was my wild pet.

"We're driving back from dinner, and we take the residential-area street, a shortcut off the main road, and Pretty Boy spies something fantastic, like a Christmas present just waiting for him to pick up. A nice juicy red Corvette.

"He had never done that before, what he was about the do, with me on board, though I have to be honest and tell you I knew what he did for a living, and he had told me all kinds of things about how the business works, how he went about what he did, so I want you to know I'm fessing up, that I'm not a babe in the woods by any means. I knew. I didn't partic-ipate, until this night, but I knew he was a car thief and good at his job.

"May I have some water?"

The nurse gave her a bottle of water, said, "Anytime you need to stop, you stop. You're my patient, and they can wait."

I glanced at the nurse. Her eyes were soft and hooded. I liked that look, and I liked the way she protected Nikki, but I hoped like hell Nikki would keep talking, damaged tongue or not. We needed to know. Manny certainly needed to know.

After swallowing some water and a pain pill, she took Leonard's hand again and continued.

"He stopped the car, said to me, 'Nikki, this will just take a minute, and then you follow me to the shop.' Right then I knew that I was on the edge of crossing over, but I got in the driver's seat, and Pretty Boy got a little bag of tools out of the trunk and crossed the street to the car.

"But things went wonky. I'm watching him, and I'll never forget, he had a kind of strut in his step. Maybe that was for me or maybe it's just how he was when he was doing something like that, because I know he loved it and had talked to me about how powerful it made him feel. He said to me, 'They think those cars are theirs until I take them, then I like to imagine how hollow they feel when they come out and there's an empty space where the car had been, and now it's my car, at least for a moment, and I feel like someone made me the king of the world, and then when I get paid, it's like money from heaven. Didn't cost me nothing more than a lock pick and a hot-wire and fine drive to the chop shop.'

"So he's standing by the driver's-side window of the Corvette, glances back at me with a smile on his face, then turns to his work, and that's when I know it's gone wrong. I didn't understand exactly what was happening at first, but then I saw a man's head raise up, and then a woman's, and I got the impression they had been parked in the drive so they could have sex. Why they parked there for that, I don't know. Maybe just for fun. Maybe not. I don't even know if that driveway was their driveway or just some random drive-way they pulled into to do something naughty. But when I saw those heads raise up, Pretty Boy jumped back liked he'd come upon a snake. I saw the man jerk the door open and step out of the car, naked.

"Pretty Boy froze with that bag of tools in his hand, and I heard the man say, 'Who the fuck are you?'

"That's when Pretty Boy dropped the bag, pulled a pistol from under his sport coat and shot twice, killing both of them. If shooting them like that wasn't cold enough, he pulled the woman's body out of the car and left both of them lying naked on the driveway. There was blood all over the concrete.

"Pretty Boy came back to his car, the pistol shots still ring-ing in my ears. He put the bag of tools in the trunk, took a towel out of the back, came to the window where I was, said, 'Don't ask a question. Follow me.'

"Lights were coming on in a house next door and some dogs had started to bark. Pretty Boy went back to the Corvette, used the towel to wipe down what I figured was blood, then he got in the car, and, using the key the man had left in the ignition, he backed out and drove down the street. I went after him, did it with the car lights off too. At the cor-ner he turned on the Corvette's lights, and I turned on mine. He turned right and I followed him.

"Part of me was thinking, Peel off, go to the cops, you're just digging yourself a grave. But, hell, I kept driving. Can I have some more water?"

The nurse helped her out, and Nikki drank long and hard from the bottle. She sighed when she handed it back.

"You need to stop and rest," the nurse said.

"No," Nikki said. "I'm fine. I want to get it all out, or as much of it as I can. I get tired, I'll write it out."

The nurse nodded. Nikki continued.

"I followed him like he asked, but I was almost in a trance. I just didn't know what else to do. We went out on the far edge of town where Larry Keith had his chop shop. All the way out there I'm thinking I've gone from being in love with a bad-boy car thief to being in love with a murderer. What do I do?

"I got to the shop and I parked out front. The shop doors were wide open. Inside it was bright. Pretty Boy drove the Corvette through the shop doors, parked, got out. I could see from where I sat that the seat of his pants was wet with blood. Then I see this guy walk up to him. I didn't know it at the time, but it was Larry Keith. Later I saw photos on the Internet, but I'll come to that. I saw Keith talking to Pretty Boy, who was explaining the blood, I guess.

"After a while, Keith, appearing none too happy, looked out the door at me in Pretty Boy's car. His expression could have curdled milk, as my mother used to say. He was a handsome guy, but even from a distance, there was something unsettling about him, like his soul was dying or was already dead. I know how that sounds, but when he looked at me, I felt like I was melting into a puddle of blood.

"Larry Keith walked Pretty Boy out of view of the doors,

and they were gone for some time, but eventually they come back into view, and Pretty Boy, I could tell that plenty was wrong, and at first I'm thinking it's the murders he committed, as he looked like someone had let the air out of him. He was almost as white as I am, walked with a kind of shuffle, like his shoes were sticking to the ground.

"The two of them walked to where I was waiting in Pretty Boy's car, and I felt sick suddenly, because Keith glanced at Pretty Boy, said so I heard it, 'We got to clean things up a little, right?'

"I wanted to think they meant the stolen car, but in that moment, I felt it meant a lot more than that. And then Keith comes over and looks in the car at me. Puts his hands on the open car window and ducks his head and looks in. I've never seen eyes that cold before, like a dead animal lying on the side of the road, its eyes open and flat and looking at nothing. He stares at me a long time, says, 'Might want to eat some red meat, honey, you look kind of pale.' I knew then I would never get the chance to eat any meat or anything else if I sat there for very long, but I was glued to the car seat, looking out the window.

"Pretty Boy walked over to the car, told me they wanted us to come inside. I was surprised they wanted me. Why? I wasn't in a stolen car. Fact was, that was the closest I'd ever come to the shop. There was something odd about the way Pretty Boy looked at me, like he was about to shovel dirt in my face. I knew then for sure that I wasn't being melodramatic, that Keith wasn't talking about 'clean up' in the sense of wiping blood off the seat of a stolen car. I was a witness to the murders, and I was connected to Pretty Boy, and he was connected to Larry Keith. I loved Pretty Boy, but I knew right then he didn't love me. I knew what was coming. Pretty Boy would have a new girl on his arm in a week, if it took that long. I'd be buried somewhere, thrown in a lake, maybe turned into a sausage or mashed up in a car crusher along with some automobile. I threw the car in gear, gunned it backward, turned it quick, and started out of there. I could hear Pretty Boy yelling for me to come back. I glanced in the rearview mirror, saw Larry Keith and a big man come out of the garage, the big man with a wrench in his hand, Pretty Boy still looking down the road at me, growing small in the rearview mirror.

"There was a flash. A bright pop of light in the mirror, and I saw Pretty Boy fold up in the middle and fall to the ground, and then I saw the big man with the wrench go to work on him. I don't know if Pretty Boy was still alive or if they were just making sure, but in a moment, I didn't see them anymore. I was driving too fast. I knew then what Pretty Boy didn't know. They hadn't planned to kill just me, they were taking him out as well. He had crossed the line from car thief to stupid. They didn't care about the murder. They cared there would be too much heat brought to bear, and they were trying to throw cold water on things before they turned into a fire. I mean, I don't know if I was thinking about it that carefully then, but that seemed like the deal to me, and I had plenty of time to think about it later. Maybe they killed him because I got away, thought he was part of that, but I think he was going to die no matter what.

"I drove wild for a while, and then I slowed down and drove on, not knowing where I was going. I only stopped to buy gas and eat a burger. Later I had to pull over and throw that burger up beside the road. It fit in my stomach like an acidic boulder. I drove through the night without plans, just reviewing what Pretty Boy had done, then what had been planned for me, and finally I kept seeing what I saw in the rearview mirror play over and over in my head. The flash of light. Pretty Boy bending in half and falling to the ground, and then that big man with the wrench.

"In the end, I drove right out of East Texas, across North Texas, crossed the Red River into eastern Oklahoma. I found a town that had its bus station beside a liquor store and parked Pretty Boy's car, a '68 Ford Mustang, out back of that store with the keys in it. I caught a bus and got off at the first stop and ended up at an out-of-the-way town about the size of a postage stamp called Hootie Hoot."

"We know it," Leonard said. "We had a little adventure there once. It makes a stretched dead rat's asshole seem like a nicer place to live."

"That proves you've been there. About half the downtown is closed and boarded off. There's a theater still there, a restaurant where they burn a bad steak and grease up worse home fries. You can gain five pounds walking by that place. It's got a few service stations and a bank and some of this and some of that, and one of the thats they had was a flower shop.

"I had a little money, and I managed to get an apartment, was quick to get a job at the flower shop. It was walking distance from where I was staying. The shop paid in cash, because even though I had some credit cards, I thought it best not to use them. I feared those men finding out who I was and tracking me. Maybe they already knew—good chance Pretty Boy told them that night before Keith came out and looked at me. I started going by the name Nikki Smith. The old man and his wife that owned the place, I think they liked the idea of someone like me, an albino, working there. It was unique in that little town, brought in a little business. You know, 'They got that albino girl over at the flower shop. Let's go over and look at her.' All I had to do to stay hidden was let the old man in the shop rub his fat hand across my ass now and again. When his wife wasn't looking, of course.

"One time, when the old lady wasn't there, he asked if the hair on my vagina was as white as the hair on my head or if I shaved it. I told him I didn't shave it because I had a disease that might get spread by shaving. I thought that might make him leave me alone. He didn't believe me, or didn't care. He kept up with the touching.

"Compared to being discovered and killed, being groped by him seemed like a small trade-off. Most of the day I made deliveries, and though I had a license, it was the one with my correct name on it, so I was extra careful. I don't know if it would have mattered had I got a ticket. I don't know if Larry Keith could track me somehow because of that. I didn't think so, but I wasn't chancing it. He had money, so he had a lot of connections. Maybe had someone looking at arrest records, checking credit card use. I know Pretty Boy once told me Larry had people in high places, moles, and he got a lot of information that way, though Pretty Boy told me it was really Larry's father that had the connections. Larry's real connection was his father, Wilson Keith. Words Pretty Boy used was 'He's the real swinging dick. Larry, he's just the underpants.'

"Anyhow, I learned how to dodge around the old man, stashed some bucks for a long jaunt to somewhere else.

"Day I left there, I was going to punch that old man as hard as I could. And I did. Hard enough to knock him down. I had to stand on a stool to do it. But before that, when I was still delivering flowers, one day I was curious, peeked at the news with the flower shop's computer. Up to then, I had managed not to bother. Didn't want to know. I knew Pretty Boy was dead, and I still loved him a little, even if he had planned to let them kill me, maybe even do it himself. I assumed he was ground up in a hot dog somewhere.

"But that day my curiosity got the better of me. Couldn't help myself. Really wasn't anything there. Nobody knew Pretty Boy was dead, didn't even know he was missing. No unknown bodies found, no one came up with a finger in a taco or some such. Then I saw another piece of news about the murder of a Nicole Beckman in Tyler. Then I knew. Someone had been hired to hunt me down and kill me, make sure I didn't talk about the chop shop, tell anything I might have learned from Pretty Boy. Thing was, someone had killed the wrong Nicole Beckman. My first thought was I was safe. They thought I was dead. My second thought was that poor girl. I felt I had to do something.

"I called the cops in Tyler, told my story. They needed to see me, of course, said they'd protect me. Wanted my testimony. On the same day I punched the old man at the flower shop as a way of delivering my resignation, the cops picked me up and hauled me to Tyler, Texas."

Nikki leaned back and shut her eyes. We all sat silent, waiting. Finally, she sat up, took the water bottle from the nurse, took another pain pill. When she started talking again, her words came slower and were tripping over each other a little, but she was determined.

"Reporters got wind of what I told the cop, about it being the wrong Nicole. Someone at the police station leaked it. News trumped common sense. They wrote how the wrong Nicole had been killed, which of course put me in even greater jeopardy. It was widely known then that I was going to be a witness for the prosecution against Larry.

"I was under protection, but I was nervous. If it had been leaked I was alive that quick and easy, I didn't know I was safe where they had put me up, a hotel downtown. Cops watching me, most of them were all right. Talked to me, played Monopoly with me, brought me books and movies, food. One night, one of those cops, he spilled some stuff to me. Not that he was supposed to, but he did, which goes to prove there are no real tight lips when it comes to rumor, gossip, or righteous news. Hell, for all I know, he was the one that let it loose to a reporter that I was alive. He liked to talk, and the thing he talked about frightened me.

"He said word was Larry Keith's dad couldn't let me stay alive. I guess it was a kind of pride thing. You don't get away from his family, not if they want you dead. And of course, there was that whole not-being-able-to-testify-if-I-was-a-corpse thing.

"This cop, Cantor was his name, he says, 'Small-time car thief and lifetime criminal Pete Ridgely got arrested for trying to boost an SUV. Minute he thought he might end up going to prison, he wanted to land as soft as he possibly could, so he decided to cut a deal. He knew who had killed the wrong Nicole: Pete, his own self.'

"That's how Cantor put it. 'Pete, his own self.' He had been paid to do the job, was so excited he got drunk, looked up Nicole Beckman in the phone book, drove to her house, and killed her. Thing was, the Nicole he wanted was me, and I was in hiding, so the wrong Nicole Beckman was murdered. Cantor said Pete told the cops, 'I don't do so good when I drink.'

"I figured his drinking had to be pretty damn bad, all right. Someone must have at some point mentioned I was Asian and albino, certainly memorable enough for those with brain cells.

"After that, Pete had his own head on the chopping block for killing the wrong girl. At that time, I was loose in the wild, so to speak, in Hootie Hoot, and Pete, he didn't know which end was up. He didn't know where to find me to make things right by killing me, and Wilson Keith wanted him dead for being a screwup, and maybe kind of wished his own son was dead for being stupid enough to hire a drunk who didn't know an albino from a rhino. Pete knew it was his turn to get whacked, so he went state's evidence. He didn't last long in jail. He had provided written testimony, but he wouldn't be speaking at the trial after all. Hanged himself."

"At least he got to quit being stupid," Leonard said.

Nikki smiled a little. It wasn't exactly an amused smile. Maybe her tongue hurt.

"Do you need to stop?" the nurse said.

Nikki gently shook her head, kept talking.

"Cantor said shortly after a jailer named Frank Quinn found Pete hanging, he retired from the jailer business and began living high on the hog without visible means of support. Turned out he liked to talk, and rumor was he talked about Pete's death now and then, like how maybe Pete got some help getting that rope around his neck.

"An explanation for Jailer Quinn's expensive lifestyle didn't happen. He was found under a piece of tin near an old fallen-down shack by two homeless men that had stopped to pee. Quinn's mouth was stuffed with his amputated foot, a symbolic suggestion he had put his foot in his mouth. Damn. I feel like I got a foot in my mouth, way my tongue is swelling."

"I said you could stop," the nurse said.

"I'm okay. At least until I'm not. May I have more water?"

The nurse gave Nikki the plastic bottle and Nikki let go of Leonard's hand and took a long pull of the water and gave the bottle back to her. She rested her head against the pillow, closed her eyes, and let whatever she was thinking about ramble around inside her head.

About the time I thought she might have fallen asleep, she opened her eyes, sighed, and picked up where she'd left off.

"Quinn had been another of Larry's hires, and now someone was cleaning up problems. Canton's guess was it was Wilson Keith doing the cleaning, or having it done, and this time by more efficient people, the cream of the crop, the High Cotton Gang, he called them."

Manny nodded. "Yeah. I know of them. Rumored team of hitters, dirty-jobbers sometimes employed by Wilson Keith, the king of East Texas dirt. Right amount of money, they'd kill their mothers."

"I was supposed to be safe, and I know Cantor was thinking he was keeping me in the loop, though he wasn't supposed to do that," Nikki said. "He had good intentions, I think. And he liked to talk. I figured I was next on the cleanup agenda."

That's when Nikki's voice began to sound as if it were coming through a potato in a sock. She had to stop. She had the nurse crank her up in her hospital bed, and she picked up the pad and pen on the table beside her and began to write. Her hand wobbled, like it was slowly being electrocuted by a weak voltage.

What she wrote in that chicken-scratch handwriting boiled down to this:

Larry's chop shop had already been shut down by the

cops. They found some violations or some such shit, but there wasn't enough evidence to have him arrested on murder charges, just Nikki's word. But it was a strong word, and there were other pieces of the puzzle that might fit together and lead to a lethal injection for Larry, and if Pete's and Quinn's deaths could be led back to Wilson Keith, that ol' boy might be having his vein tapped with a spike as well. But to clinch the deal, to get them both, Nikki's testimony was just the thing. But she had to make it to trial, and it was reasonably certain someone at the cop shop in Tyler was leaking to Keith and cashing a check. Someone with all the ethics of that jailer who'd ended up with enough money to retire. Maybe whoever it was ought to have thought deeper, remembered how the jailer turned out, rotting under a piece of hot tin.

Cops hid Nikki out in the deep woods between LaBorde and San Augustine, but the one thing wrong with it was that someone, or more than one, in law enforcement was on the Keith payroll. Nikki wrote:

They knew where I was, where the cop protecting me, Cantor, was. It wasn't an accident they found me in those woods. Someone squealed, and certainly for money. Place where we were, a cabin, the toilet got stopped up, and I had to go, so I went outside to pee in the woods like some kind of wild animal, and then the real wild animals showed up. Cantor was inside working on the toilet, and there I was outside, peeing in the dark woods, with a storm brewing, feeling pretty safe, and the killers came. I heard a shot from the cabin. That would have been poor Cantor taking a bullet. Then I saw them coming along the trail, wearing night-vision goggles, carrying guns.

I panicked, ran, but they caught me, held me down and used a pair of tin snips on my tongue. One held my head, another pulled down my chin, and then this little guy used the snips.

My guess was that was Kung Fu Rabbit.

I think they planned to get the whole tongue to take back to the Keiths. Symbolic stuff about me not being able to testify. But the little guy snipped quick and I was struggling. Hurt like holy hell. I passed out. And then they got me up and pushed me against a tree, were going to do the tongue business again, get it right, put a bullet in my head or a knife in my gut, but there was a loud crack in the woods, a tree breaking and falling, and in that moment, they wheeled and that limb landed right in the middle of us, knocked the little guy with the snips to the ground. I broke loose and ran, shots dancing around me.

I was a track star in high school, and I can still run. I got some space between us quick, leaped over a pile of briars and rolled down a deep embankment and landed in a ditch full of water. Then I was out of that and running. They fired down at me, but the night and me running, all the brush, kept them from hitting me.

I was growing weak. It was hard to breathe. I had to spit blood constantly. My tongue was swelling. I was starting to stumble, felt faint.

I came through the woods out onto the highway, and soon as I did, there they came. They had me figured. I could see their lights coming down a little road next to the woods that emptied into the highway.

I ran out into the highway, thinking I had to get across and into the woods on that side. Maybe not really thinking at all. Just trying to get away. And then you guys showed up. Another minute or two, they would have had me.

That's where she ended it. She gave the pad to me and lay back against her pillow again.

24

By the time we got all of the story from Nikki, she was tuckered from talking and writing, and she had to take her medicine. The nurse handled that, and we went into Hanson's office with Manny. She sat behind his desk. As always, I noted just how fine-looking she was. Even the scar along the side of her face gave her a uniqueness, like a model who had been in a knife fight.

She said, "Well, you believe that story?"

"It sounds possible," I said.

"Yeah," she said. "It's too outlandish to be made up, and she tells it straight, writes it out straight. I believe it. I mean, hell, she may be protecting herself a bit here and there, and I'm thinking she might actually have helped Pretty Boy steal a few cars, but I don't know if that's true or if that's just the cop in me talking. Do this awhile, you forget not everyone has an angle. Not everyone is trying to get away with something, and not everyone is lying. Lies are saved for presidents and Congress."

"Everyone lies," Leonard said, "and all the time."

"Not everyone has a murder to lie about," I said. "I believe her."

"She seems to trust you two," Manny said.

"We could be being used," Leonard said.

"You really think so?" I said. "Hell, you dragged her hurt ass out of the rain."

"Naw, I guess she's telling the truth. Mostly. Like Manny said, I think maybe she not only knew what Pretty Boy was doing, but she might have been helping him do it."

"At this point," Manny said, "none of that matters. What matters is the big fish, so we have to take care of her, make sure she testifies. You guys mind sticking around? I'm going to see if I can verify what she told us, check out a few things. She might still prefer you two being here if I need to talk to her some more, and I'm sure I will."

"We're at your service," Leonard said, "long as you have something to eat."

"Go to the break room. There's some snacks there, coffee, nothing special."

"We've had the cop shop's hospitality before," I said. "We know what we're in for. Potato chips and bad coffee."

"Get tired, use one of the cells to lie down. We aren't exactly packing them in, and with all the storming, I doubt we will be. Even the weasels hunker down in weather like this."

Me and Leonard went into the break room and poured coffee so sour and acidic you could have used it to melt a hole through a vault. There weren't any potato chips, but there were some stale peanut butter crackers. We sat at the break table, sipped our bad coffee, ate our crackers, and felt forlorn.

Outside, the storm had regained its intensity. It just wouldn't go away. It would blow out, then blow back, and now the wind was howling and the rain was beating and my soul was quivering. There was something almost apocalyptic about that storm.

Manny came into the break room, said, "It's a wet hell out there. Lot of patrol cars can't get back to the station. Water's rising. I kid you not, I heard from dispatch there are people in boats cruising around where roads and highways used to be. Boys, you aren't going home tonight, and I'm not sure about tomorrow either. Supposed to get worse."

The lights flickered.

"We have a backup generator," Manny said. "Also, there's that pie Alton left for the station. Chocolate mousse pie."

"You took a peek?" Leonard said.

"Yeah, I looked. He always brings something different."

The pie was in a little refrigerator where the cops kept some personal food. Manny took it out of there and placed it on the table and opened the box.

The pie smelled delightful and my mouth began to water.

"You know, Alton is not going to get to taste this pie," she said. "Not even one piece, and I know that's mean and breaking his rule, but hey, we're trapped here. I'll take the hit for it, and I'll buy him a whole pie. But tonight, we are the pie-eaters of doom."

"Pie confiscation," I said.

"Absolutely," Manny said.

"What about the nurse?" I said.

"We won't tell her," Manny said. "Or the dispatchers, or Nikki, and she can't eat it anyway, right?"

"Right," Leonard said.

We split the pie in thirds with a plastic knife, put it on paper plates, ate it with plastic forks, and drank more bad coffee. When we finished, Leonard said, "Thank you, Alton, wherever you may be."

"He's on the street," Manny said. "We've lost a lot of the old crew lately, resignations, people moving, and right now some people are on vacation. Bad time for this storm to hit. Currently, some of our force is out in the hinterlands. Now they're trapped, cut off, can't get back to the station. Some can't even leave their homes and get to work to begin with. Lake LaBorde has grown so large the whole western side of town is an enormous lake. The dam isn't looking too good out there either. It may not hold. The east side isn't much better. Water is seeping out of creeks and swamps, and the water has closed the roads. Now they got a hurricane coming into the Gulf, and they think it's going to hit us with more rain, and we may just get a direct piece of that windy monster. To make matters worse, weather people say it'll stall here for a while."

"Damn," Leonard said.

The idea of all that water inching toward us gave me the creeps. I began to worry about my family. I stepped out of the office to call Brett to see if she had decided to haul everyone off to Tyler. I wanted to tell her our situation, what we were up to, but there was no cell service.

When I came back into the break room, I said, "Leonard, try your phone."

He did. Nothing.

Manny tried her cell with the same lack of results.

"They can't repair things fast enough," Manny said. "Tower's down is my guess."

The lights blinked.

"So, if the electricity goes, does the generator cut on automatically?" Leonard said.

"It does, if we get to that situation, and I suspect we may," Manny said.

"I'm going to see a man about a horse," I said.

I thought I'd make a bathroom trip, then use the cop-shop ground line to call Brett. I walked along the hall to the bathroom. The place was quiet and eerie as a politician's soul. There were only a few people in the station. The three of us, Nikki, the nurse, the receptionist, couple cops, three dispatchers.

As I walked by the dispatch room, one of the dispatchers was going in, having made her own bathroom trip, I suppose. The door closed slowly behind her. I didn't hear them answering calls in there. Maybe the landlines were out too, though I knew they had serious backup that most of the town wouldn't have.

I went to the bathroom, washed up, walked out, and went to Nikki's cell. She was up but groggy. The nurse was helping her to the bathroom, holding on to the rack with the juice in it, rolling it along.

"I thought you were knocked out," I said to Nikki.

"Light dosage," the nurse said. "But she'll go right back to sleep soon as she gets back to bed."

Nikki smiled at me. It was a drunk kind of smile.

They went on to the ladies' room, and I went to the back door of the station, pushed it open. It wouldn't open from the outside unless you knew the code to use on the exterior keypad. That was comforting.

The air that hit me was cool and sticky. It lifted my hair and shirt collar. It was dark as the source of sin out there, except for occasional rips of lightning. In those flashes, I could see water running wild over the concrete, and where the street dipped down a bit to the left, it was like a little stream. In the flashes, the water was the color of a vein of silver.

I wondered if we might be able to get home. It was wet and dangerous, but if we went to the right, on up to North Street, we might manage to turn on Main and make it to the house. But then below Main was the creek, and it filled easy, rose up over the bridge, so maybe not. I was thinking about us trying it in spite of what Manny said. Perhaps this was the time, before things got even worse. I wanted to see my family. If I got home and things got so bad we couldn't get out, at

least I would be with them, and Nikki wouldn't be going anywhere anyway, not until the storm played out and the roads
were cleared.

I took a deep breath of the wet air, let the door close, made
sure it was locked, and walked back to the break room. It was
then that the wind outside screamed and the rain fell on the
roof like hippos dropped from a plane. The building actually
shook.

All hell was about to break loose.

25

We sat around awhile, tried to talk about this and that, but that wind howling and that rain slamming made it difficult.

Finally, I said to Manny, "I'm going to take you up on that offer to lie down."

"Other than the one Nikki's in, the cells are open," she said. "Pick one."

"We've been here before," I said, "and in a different capacity. We've got familiarity."

Leonard said, "I'm out too. That coffee didn't do shit for me. I'm starting to see dancing tigers. Going to bed. I'd like my breakfast on a tray with a little rose in a white vase in the morning."

"Yeah, that's going to happen," Manny said.

Me and Leonard walked out together, down the hall, turned past where Nikki and the nurse were, found a two-bunk cell, went in, left the door open, took off our shoes, and stretched out on the bunks.

"I have never liked storms," Leonard said.

"I know."

"Think it'll pass quickly?"

"No. This one is going to hang around awhile. You heard Manny."

"She doesn't know everything."

"And I do?"

"You're right," Leonard said. "You don't know shit either."

I'd thought, as tired as I was, I would probably lie down and then the coffee would hit and I'd be sleepy but wouldn't be able to sleep, and I'd feel miserable. Too much coffee bothered me that way.

This didn't prove to be the case.

As my head hit that thin little pillow, I had a brief moment where I listened to the wind and the rain, and then I fell into a light sleep, one of those kinds where you are aware of where you are and yet part of you is in the night world. I remember I had a strange near-awake dream about a pack of wild dogs walking across high water like Jesus hounds, their fangs bared. The moon was bright behind them, and then the moon seemed to fall off a shelf and hit the water in a gold explosion, and then I was deep asleep.

I'm not sure how long I slept because I didn't check my watch when I woke up. Leonard was still snoozing. The lights in the corridor were flickering as if they were having a fit of some kind.

I got up and put my shoes on, walked down the hall to the bathroom. I went back and checked on Nikki and the nurse. The nurse was asleep in her chair, her head hung down, her nurse hat on the nightstand on top of the books.

Nikki lay in bed, unmoving, the IV in her arm, the IV bag in a rack next to her. Her white hair was spread out against the white pillow; a white sheet was pulled over her pale body. The shadows from the cell bars lay over her and the nurse like long bruises.

I padded down the hall, past the dispatch office, went into the break room, and got a new cup of bad coffee and a packet of peanut butter crackers. I made my way through one stale cracker, then the rest of them, along with the coffee, went into the trash.

I walked to Hanson's office. The door was open. Manny was leaned back in Hanson's chair, asleep.

I started back to the break room, but when I came to it, I kept walking. Now that I was awake, I was too wired to go in there and sit. I was like a bored child with no one to play with.

I walked along to the door that led to the foyer. There was a glass-and-wire frame in the door that led out to it. You went out, the door locked behind you. You had to be buzzed back in. I was thinking I might go out and walk around in the wide foyer, perhaps poke my head outside and look at the street from the front of the station, but I didn't want to be locked out.

I decided to walk through the back door to the receptionist's station and ask if it would be all right for me to go out

137

front for a moment and have her buzz me back in. Maybe she and I could visit a bit to knock the boredom down.

I went in carrying my coffee, and the woman there, pleasant-faced, her hair tied back, dressed in blue jeans, boots, and a loose shirt, smiled at me. She looked fit, muscular.

I didn't know her. But there was something familiar about her.

"This weather," she said. "Really something, huh?"

"Yep," I said.

There was a long canvas bag at her feet, and the door into the foyer was cracked open, held in position by a brick. I had never seen them do that before. It was always locked. The closet to the right was leaking dark water under the door.

"Can I get you some coffee?" I said.

"Maybe later," she said. She swiveled in her chair and looked at me directly. She had a coat stretched across her knees.

"Are you new?" I said.

"I am. Came on shift a little while ago."

I nodded. "Well, all right. Hang in there."

I went out and closed the door and walked to the break room and poured my coffee into the sink. I picked up a chair and brought it back and tilted it under the door handle to the receptionist's office.

I made my way back to the door that was used to buzz visitors in, examined it. No way to put a chair under that. There was only a push bar on my side.

Quickly, I walked to where Manny was, shoved the door wide, and called her name.

She opened her eyes with tremendous effort. When she got them open, she glared at me.

"You better have fresh doughnuts and coffee or I'm going to shoot you."

"Let me ask you something. Do you have a new receptionist?"

"What?"

"Do you have a new receptionist?"

"Just Evelyn for this time of night. And I figure, like the rest of us, she's trapped here for a while. Now, unless you want to know who all is on the day shift, I have to ask: What the hell, Hap?"

"Evelyn seems to have been replaced, and the new woman's propped open her office door, one that leads to the foyer."

"That's against regulations."

"Figured it was."

Manny studied me for a moment, then opened the desk drawer, took out a couple lightweight revolvers. She came around the desk and handed them to me.

"I have a feeling I'm deputized," I said.

"Go wake Leonard."

26

I quickstepped down to the cell, and when I got there Leonard was sitting on the edge of the bed, pulling on his shoes.

He looked at the guns I was carrying, one in each hand.

"I snore that bad."

"Something isn't right," I said.

He finished with his shoes, and we went along the corridor after looking in on Nikki and the nurse. They were still asleep and fine.

We hustled down the hall, found Manny standing outside the receptionist door. She had moved the chair I had placed there.

She said to me, "You're backup if needed."

"What about me?" Leonard said.

"You're a man without a gun."

I gave Leonard the extra pistol.

I eased to the side of the door with Leonard. Manny opened it, left it open, and went in. I could see the "new receptionist" through the crack in the open door, where the hinges met the wall. She still had the coat stretched over her lap, and her hand was under it.

Manny said, "Odd, I don't recognize you."

"I'm a replacement," I heard her say.

"I don't think you are," Manny said. "Not a proper one, anyway. What you holding under that coat, girl?"

The woman's face turned sour. "My clit," she said.

"I bet mine's bigger," Manny said.

That's when the woman moved and the coat slid off her lap and her hand came out. It wasn't her clit at all. It was a big old nasty automatic with a fat silencer on the end of it. The gun huffed once.

Manny moved. It didn't seem fast, didn't seem an excited move. She merely lifted her pistol and fired. It was really loud inside that room. Her shot hit the woman in the face and her head went back, and then I couldn't see her anymore because she had fallen out of the chair.

Me and Leonard entered in the office behind Manny. Manny was replacing her gun in its holster. I had the one she gave me held down by my side.

The woman lay on the floor. Her head was a mess. Her gun had slid across the tile and ended up against the wall. A cell phone was beside her, having also fallen out from under the coat. There was blood everywhere, even on the great sheet of plasti-glass that fronted the receptionist's area. Manny's bullet had gone through the woman's head and hit it. It had made only a small dent. That was some plastic.

I knew then where I had seen that woman. She had been part of the crew that had tried to kill Nikki, not to mention me and Leonard. Hers was the face I had seen in the lightning flash when we were at the cabin.

I went over and kicked away the brick holding the door open. The door closed automatically.

"How'd she get in?" I said. "And where's Evelyn?"

Leonard went over to the closet, where the dark liquid was running out from under the door in a broader and more recognizable pool than before. He opened the door. I saw Evelyn inside. She was sitting on the floor with her head on her knees. She was leaking a lot of blood from her ear. The inside of the closet smelled like heated copper. She wasn't sleeping. I thought of all those photos of her family on her desk, and felt sick.

"Somehow, this bitch," Manny said, looking down at the woman she had shot, "convinced Evelyn to let her in. That door is pretty solid, and the lock is good."

"Maybe she beat the lock, the keypad code," Leonard said. "People can do that."

"Damn," Manny said. "Evelyn was all right. What the hell?"

"Nikki," I said. "They've come for her. And considering the weather, they must want her bad. Someone, Daddy Keith is my guess, is paying some serious bucks to get rid of her."

It sort of came together then. The woman Manny had

killed had managed to talk her way into the receptionist's office, maybe used some kind of sob story. Or maybe she shot Evelyn through the little speaker hole in the glass, dragged her into the closet, and cleaned the blood up a little before she took her place.

However it had been managed, it had been managed.

Seemed to me her next step would have been to let some coconspirators in. Folks who could deal with the cops, dispatchers, all of us. Leaving no witnesses, including the most valuable one to the Tyler Police Department's case.

"I'm going to take a look outside," Manny said. "Close the door behind me, and unless it's me, and just me, don't open it again."

"Hey," Leonard said, "you're what law there is here. You got to stay around to handle things. I'll take a look."

Manny thought on that. "I don't know," she said.

"I'm going," he said.

Before Manny could think on it anymore, Leonard was out of the reception door, clutching the pistol. Me and Manny stood by the glass and watched as Leonard eased across the foyer to the front door, pushed the exit bar, then slowly stuck his head outside into the wild weather.

The wind came whistling in, slipped through the talk-hole gap in the plasti-glass, hit us inside the reception room. The air was damp and wet and cold, like the skin of a drowned person.

Leonard eased out farther into the storm, and soon most of him was no longer in sight. We could see his hand, which was holding the door open. Water was rushing in around his feet, washing over his boots.

He came back quickly and the front door closed behind him. I opened the inside door and let him in.

He had a look on his face like someone had borrowed his dick and forgotten to give it back.

"Well?" Manny said.

"Things are bad."

27

The parking lot is nothing but water," he said. "Worse, there are people in a fucking armored car out where Highway Seven used to be. There were some people wearing water boots and slickers sitting on top of cars. Sitting there with the rain pounding on them. They have guns. They were pointed at me. Pretty sure they're the same assholes that tried to kill Nikki in the woods, plus others. Though they are missing one now."

He looked at the body on the floor.

"Armored car?" I said.

"Yeah. SUV all tricked out. Got a winch and shit on it, probably holds five or so, has a boat trailer on the back and there's a motorboat in it. The car is about halfway submerged, but it looks like it could plow through some pretty deep and fast water. Speaking of water, it's two feet high and rising. There's a dump truck parked on the far side of the street, and there's a garbage truck too. That's not where those are kept, is it?"

"Nope," Manny said.

"I think they got them some special rides," Leonard said. "Makeshift tanks borrowed from the sanitation and street departments. Drivers would be sitting high in those things, could navigate this bad water a lot better than in cars."

Manny picked up the dead woman's coat, popped it out, and placed it over the corpse. "Shit," Manny said. "I killed that woman."

"Yeah, she ain't gonna get no deader," Leonard said.

"I felt like I had no choice."

"Drop it, sis," Leonard said. "We've got our asses in a crack here, so feel bad about it later, and when I'm home. I don't want to hear it."

"It's not the first time I've shot someone," Manny said.

"There you are," Leonard said. "Now you've had more practice. And she's still the bitch you thought she was before, only she's a dead bitch. And you should check your ear."

Manny reached up, brought away her hand with blood on the fingertips. "My earring is gone."

"Silent shot," Leonard said. "Clipped your earring. Had she been a better shot or faster, you'd be on the floor instead of her. You did all right."

Manny took a deep breath, went where the receptionist had sat, reached under the little counter in front of the voice hole, and flipped a switch. The automatic front-door lock clicked. Water was running under the door now, and that was a tightly framed door.

A moment passed, and then there was a push against the door, but the door held.

"Good timing," I said.

"That'll hold them for now," Leonard said.

"This is a police station," Manny said. "They're assaulting a police station. This is absurd."

"And except for you, there are no police here," I said. "Just the dispatchers and some citizens. Maybe it's not that absurd."

Leonard gave me back the pistol I had given him, picked up the dead woman's gun, unscrewed the silencer, and tossed it onto the floor.

"I want those motherfuckers to hear me coming," he said.

We went back into the main station, letting the door to the receptionist's room close. I put the chair back under the latch so I could pretend it was another barrier, but considering these guys had commandeered a dump truck and a garbage truck and had brought a fucking boat, it didn't seem like something that would stop them for long.

Manny's boot heels clicked as she walked along the hallway, and we followed her. She used a key card to unlock a metal door. It was a roomful of weapons and body armor.

"Suit up," she said.

It was the police arsenal.

Most of the weapons were high-powered pieces of busi-ness. I decided on a twelve-gauge pump shotgun and an automatic rifle. I put on a bulletproof vest and traded in the gun Manny had given me for a large-caliber revolver.

Leonard loaded up with a serious shoot-'em-up automatic rifle and two handguns, including the one from the dead woman. He also put on a vest.

Manny took an automatic rifle and another handgun and put on a vest. She gave each of us shells for the weapons and a kind of slip-over jumper that had numerous pockets for shells.

We loaded the weapons and packed the remaining boxes of shells into those jumper pockets.

There were some rain slickers in there too, and they were better than the ones we owned, so we took them, went ahead and put them on. I had a feeling we were all going to end up outside in the rain.

All of this was done quickly.

Manny went down the hall to the dispatch room to prepare them for what might happen. She punched the code and went inside. Me and Leonard hurried down the hall to where Nikki and the nurse were sleeping.

Just before we reached the cell, when we came even with the short hall that led to the back door, we heard the automatic lock on it click open.

28

Damp air blasted through the doorway as it widened, and then we saw Alton. At first, I was much relieved, and then I saw his service weapon in his hand and the stone-cold look on his face, and I knew sure as shit stinks, Alton was bought and sold.

I could see behind him two other armed men, both holding serious long guns. I didn't recognize either of them. Alton came in lifting his weapon, startled at seeing us as much as we were startled at seeing him and suddenly knowing on which side he stood. I whirled with the shotgun, pumped a round into place, crouched low, and cut loose.

At the same time, I heard Leonard's automatic rifle bark, and I was reasonably certain it was a miss, because they all kept coming. Thinking Alton probably had on an armored vest, I shot low and took out his knees. It was like he had fallen over a trip wire. His head came forward and his legs went backward, into the doorway.

I got a glimpse of the two other men that were now in the doorway, and then there was a sound like two pans being banged together. I saw one of the men lose half his face, due to Leonard's second shot making good, and behind me a shot slapped into the wall and sent plaster flying up and snowing down on me.

I pumped another round, and the last man standing, the one who had sent a shell into the wall behind me, got a load from my shotgun. The blast hit him in the neck, and he went straight to the ground, so fast it seemed as if a hole had opened beneath him. He fell onto the concrete platform outside the door; the rain washed his blood away as fast as it gushed out of him. He raised one hand and made a movement akin to someone flagging a ride, and then he caught one—the bus to hell. His hand fell down, trembled slightly, and he was still.

Leonard was already dragging Alton away from the door, letting it close. Alton would have been the one with the key code, but I figured he might have given it to one of the others, and that was a sincere worry. If he hadn't given it to anyone else, then in time, if Keith's crew were as well equipped as they seemed, they were coming through that door, one way or another.

Leonard rolled Alton over on the tile, which was turning wet and dark with blood. My shot had taken out his legs. They were just raw bone and shattered flesh hanging together by frayed strands of muscle. Alton was still alive.

"Piece of shit," Leonard said.

"Needed the money," Alton said.

"Piece of shit," Leonard said again.

Alton managed a smile. It seemed strange there on that pained face, or maybe he was past pain right then. Maybe it wasn't a smile but a clenching of teeth.

"Wish I hadn't done it," he said.

"I bet," Leonard said. "And just for the record, I ate your slice of that goddamn heavenly pie."

Alton laughed blood onto his lips.

"Of course you did," he said.

Alton stared at both of us as if straining to see us from a great distance, and then what was left of Alton's life left him with a burst of air and a violent tremble. The blood beneath him pooled wider.

"What the hell was he thinking?" Leonard said.

"I bet he was thinking about his sick kid," I said.

"Well, he might as well have been thinking about dog shit, because he can't do a damn thing for her now."

Behind us we heard footsteps. I pumped a round in the shotgun and turned.

It was Manny hastily making her way toward us.

29

Manny saw Alton on the floor, said, "They got him, those bastards."

"Wrong bastards," I said.

I saw the realization wash over her face. "You guys shot Alton?"

"Technically, Hap did," Leonard said.

"He switched sides," I said.

"We'd been a second slower, him and his two buddies, who are now holding down the wet concrete outside, would have come in," Leonard said.

"Alton has the lock code," she said.

"Had," Leonard said.

"Damn you, Alton," she said.

"Remember he brought us a good pie, and let his memory go," Leonard said.

"Do you think he might have given the code to the others?" she said.

"Probably not," I said. "That would have meant they didn't need him at all. Knowing the code and not telling them could have been his trump card. Then again, what do I know?"

"Believe him," Leonard said. "He doesn't know much."

We saw the nurse then, peeking around the corner of the cell section. From there she could see us but not what was down that short hall, the one where Alton lay in a puddle of blood.

"It's all right," Manny said as we hustled toward the nurse. "But we are going to have to make some tough decisions."

"Tough decisions?" she said.

"Is Nikki awake?" I asked.

The nurse nodded. "She's groggy, but awake. We heard gunfire."

"You did indeed," Manny said. "Come on, let's get Nikki."

As we hurried into the cell block, Manny said, "I gave the dispatchers guns, told them to stay inside the dispatch room. They aren't cops, though, aren't professional shooters, so the ones outside get into the station, it's only a matter of time before they break into the dispatch office."

"Let's hope it doesn't come to that," I said.

As we reached Nikki's cell, Leonard said one of his favorite sayings. "Hope in one hand, shit in the other, see which one fills up first."

30

The nurse unhooked the IV bag from Nikki, and then we had them moving. We guided them down the hall to the dispatch office, Nikki kind of stumbling along, about half doped up. Manny knocked at the dispatch door. It was a couple of knocks, followed by a series. Code she had given them.

One of the men, a guy with longer hair than you would expect on someone working for dispatch, opened the door. Manny went inside with the nurse and Nikki. We stood outside the room and waited.

Manny came out. "She's safer there, at least for now."

That's when we heard a clacking sound in the hallway, a voice. We followed the sound, came back to Alton's body, which was leaking even more blood, like a spilled can of red paint.

Leonard, careful not to get too much blood on his shoes,

bent down, patted Alton's coat pocket, found a little walkie-talkie, old-school. Leonard fished it out.

Leonard touched the walkie, turned on the speaker.

Leonard said, "Hello, Pippo's Pizza Parlor."

"Who do I have?" a voice on the other end said.

"Well," Leonard said, "it ain't Alton."

"Ah," said the voice. "I'm assuming Alton met with a bad end."

"You could say that," Leonard said. "You can also mark the two that were with him off your Christmas-card list."

"I see. Well, I'm going to assume you're the black guy. You sound like a black guy."

"You sound like an asshole," Leonard said. "But I'm going to assume you're Wilson Keith."

The voice on the other end laughed. "You know, I know who you are. You're Leonard, and Hap's there, and that cute little cop piece, Manuela, is there with you as well."

Alton had given him that information, of course. I wished then I could shoot him again. I was glad we didn't save him any pie.

"We just want the girl, then we go," said the voice.

"That's it? You don't want maybe some coffee first, little hand job?"

"We just want the girl."

"Yeah," Leonard said. "What we want is better insurance, some new clothes, and a trip to anywhere but here, but I don't think that's happening."

"Leonard," said the voice. "That sounds practiced."

"A little. I like to have some quips on hand. Sometimes I say things over and over, I like them so much. Here's one now: You're an asshole."

"Alton said you two thought you were smart guys."

"Maybe not that smart, but smart enough not to give you the girl and expect a free ride out of here."

"I can see why you might not trust me, but I think we should talk."

"Aren't we talking?"

"I mean in person."

"So you can shoot us?"

"You could shoot me. What say you to this? I come to you, through the front door, but I bring in one of my guys, and we work this out."

"We can't work this out."

"Might be a way we all go home happy."

"I'm not seeing that," Leonard said.

"What's it hurt to talk?"

"I don't trust you."

"Fair enough. But it might be productive for all of us."

We were all listening to this. Manny leaned in to Leonard, whispered something.

Leonard nodded, clicked the walkie. "All right," Leonard said. "You come in through the front door in five, not before that, and you can have a guy at the door, but he can't carry a weapon."

"I would be taking all the chances here. So what about this? You stay behind the reception glass, we'll talk through the voice hole, and my guard carries a weapon in case things go south. You can have weapons too. Fair?"

"All right. You stay on your side, us on ours, but the body-guard at the door can't be carrying a big weapon. He can have a handgun, holstered, put away. We'll do the same."

There was silence on the other end for a long moment. Then: "Place me a chair out front of the reception glass. I like to be comfortable. Maybe some bourbon."

"A chair we got, bourbon we don't," said Leonard. "Maybe I could just piss in a jar for you."

"The chair will do."

31

W e could just shoot him in the head," Leonard said, "guy at the door too."

"I don't think so," Manny said. "He still has people outside, and maybe a second in command. His son may be out there."

"Larry sounds like the one we'd rather deal with," Leonard said. "He's not as bright. But the dad, he sounds like trouble. Crafty-ass shit on a stick. Kind of guy thinks he can talk his way out of anything and talk you into anything, along with providing a lot of goddamn money. I hate that type. I wish I had money out the ass like that. I did, you and me would retire, Hap. Well, I would. Maybe I could give you a light allowance or something."

"What we're doing here is stalling for time," Manny said. "I have an idea that might help us out, but we got to get our Mr. Asshole to chat awhile."

"Have Hap talk to him," Leonard said. "He's chatty."

"This is true," I said.

"Thing is, with the water rising and them knowing exactly where we and Nikki are, this place won't be safe. They'll get in, and we'll be trapped like rats."

"Okay," I said, "what's the idea?"

She told us. It wasn't that great, but considering our circumstances, hiding under one of the jail-cell bunks was beginning to look like our only other option. This idea of hers, well, it was something.

While me and Manny talked with him, stalling for time, Leonard was to take the others to the old transport bus and start it up. That didn't sound all that good, but there was one advantage to it: There was a hidden exit that led into the compound yard. The bus was about twenty feet away from the back door.

Thing was, we then had to have enough time for Manny and myself to get on the bus. And then once we roared out of there, if we made it that far, we had to worry about outpacing them and not getting caught in deep water.

Piece of cake.

Though, actually, I would have preferred another piece of that chocolate mousse pie, no guns, a nice warm house, and a foot massage from my one and only.

32

Before me and Manny went into the receptionist's office with the walkie-talkie, Leonard said, "Don't let anything go wrong. Just keep him engaged."

"That's all? Don't let anything go wrong?" I said. "What could go wrong?"

"Remember, this is us."

"Yeah," I said. "That means most anything could go wrong."

"I'll wait on you."

"Don't wait any longer than we've talked about waiting. You go when you should go. Don't worry about me."

"How can I not? You're so incompetent."

"Yeah, but I have my charm to fall back on."

"You better have that pistol instead of your charm."

"Listen, Leonard. Me and Manny, we're not out there on time, you head out."

"You think I'd wait on your ass?"

Manny was bringing everyone out of the dispatch room right then. She hustled them down the corridor, and Leonard waved them to him, and away they went, my brother heading out into the unknown, a pack of ducklings behind him. Except one.

The long-haired guy.

Manny said, "Jordan, you know what you got to do?"

"I think so," he said.

"No thinking so," she said. "You go into the generator room and in fifteen minutes from when I say 'Mark,' you do what I told you to do, then you go out the back door and run to the bus like your ass is on fire. Do not mess around."

"I don't plan to."

"Here's a flashlight for when the lights go out."

Jordan took it. I saw him take a long breath like he was about to jump into deep water, and with the weather the way it was, he just might be doing that.

Manny looked at me. "You ready?"

"I am. Hearing Keith on the walkie, I think he's a guy likes to talk, same as me. His plan is to wear us down with fear, make us give up and give him the girl, so I think it'll be easy to keep him talking."

Manny turned back to Jordan. "You got a watch?"

"Phone. Well, it's nothing but a clock now."

"What time you got?"

He told her. She adjusted her watch. He held up his phone and they compared timepieces.

"Mark," she said.

"Mark," he said.

"Okay," she said. "Get into position."

Jordan nodded, started down the hall.

Manny handed me a small flashlight. "I have one too. Put it in your slicker. You're going to need it."

I looked down the long hall and saw Leonard and the others standing in front of the door to the back lot, waiting.

Leonard gave us a thumbs-up.

I nodded at him.

"All right," Manny said, "let's play the game and hope the prize isn't a bullet in our heads."

33

I was all right until we went through the door into the receptionist's room, and then the fear hit me. My legs trembled and my mouth felt dry and tasted of copper. Me and Leonard had been in plenty of tight spots, but we were braver when we were together. At least I was. Leonard probably did okay either way.

I think what was scaring me more than my own possible demise was that my brother Leonard might be killed. It had been close a few times, for both of us, but if something happened to him, no matter how much I loved Brett and my daughter, Chance, I had to wonder if I could make it. It would be worse than losing an arm. Family breathes for each other, and close family breathes as one.

I took a deep breath and propped the door we had come through open so we could make a fast retreat into the station.

We put the long guns just to the outside of the reception room, leaning them against the wall. We took off the slickers, not wanting Keith to see them and think we were ready to hit the great outdoors, and dropped them on the floor next to the wall.

The lights were adjustable in the office, so Manny turned them down a bit so we wouldn't look like moths against a lightbulb. I found a chair like Keith asked for, went out of the reception room into the wide foyer, and put the chair there, about four feet from the plasti-glass.

"Comes through that door," she said, "nothing says he won't come through shooting. He may not come through at all, but some of his goons might, and not to talk."

"Keith will show up, all right."

"Because you trust his word?"

"Because of what I already said. I trust his ego. He believes anyone can be cajoled into anything, bought out, intimidated, what have you. I'm counting on that."

"Yeah, you do keep saying that."

"And I keep believing it."

Manny nodded at me, turned on the walkie Leonard had given her. "You out there?"

Static, then a voice. "I'm at the door. Unlock it."

"You come through in a rush or there's a pack of you, we'll be gone before you can get to the reception glass."

"My bodyguard will come in first. No long weapons, but she'll be armed, a three-eighty in her holster. She's ready to go if it comes to that."

"So are we," Manny said. She clipped the walkie to her belt, reached under the desk, and flipped the door-lock switch. We stood with our hands near our pistols.

There was a moment of hesitation, and then the door opened slowly. The bodyguard came in. She was short and stout and moved like a cat. She pushed a rain hood off her head. Her dark hair was tied back. She had hard features beaded with water and a look on her face that almost made me think she had laser vision.

She stepped to the side and Keith came in. He wore a black rain slicker but no hood. The slicker was made like a cowboy duster and fell low to his ankles. He had on a cowboy hat with a transparent blue plastic cover over it. He was tall and looked Native American. He was probably sixty, but a good, solid sixty. He had on black cowboy boots, the toes of which were all I could see beneath the slicker. He took off the hat and flicked it a little, sending rainwater into the foyer. He gave the hat to the woman and she accepted it without taking her eyes off us. She held the hat in one hand, the gun in the other.

Keith unzipped the slicker and took his time slipping out of it. He handed that to the bodyguard as well. He took his hat back and put it on. Under the slicker, he had on a pair of black jeans and a light black jacket. It was unzipped, and a black shirt was visible. It had silver snap pockets and silver snaps where buttons would be. He looked as comfortable as a pimp in a whorehouse.

He walked over and sat in the chair. The woman stayed

next to the door, just in case Keith wanted her to hold his hat again.

Manny hit the switch under the counter, and the door lock snicked. The bodyguard touched the butt of her .380.

"Is that wise?" Keith said. He had a nice voice, like a radio announcer's.

"Just keeping things honest," Manny said. "Tell her to take her hand off the gun."

Keith looked back at the woman, nodded. The woman put the gun away.

The chair he was sitting in was a tall chair, so he was looking directly at us. He crossed his legs, then reached out and pulled his pants leg down slightly. Manny took a seat in the receptionist chair, and I stood at her side, one hand near my gun, the other on the back of her chair.

"This really can be easy," Keith said.

"Can it?" Manny said.

"It certainly can. It's a simple thing you need to do, and you do that, then both of you walk away."

"I think I know what that simple thing is, and I'm not going to do it," Manny said.

"Look, I respect honor. I do. But the truth is, this isn't a comic book, this isn't the sort of thing where everything is black or white. The world has a lot of gray."

"I agree," Manny said, "but some things aren't that gray. And there's that whole law-and-order issue. I'm a cop."

"So was Alton, but, like you, he had bills to pay. He wasn't a bad guy, just knew how to do business. Is that so bad, taking care of your family?"

"Depends on how you pay those bills," Manny said. "And you know what? He paid a big bill tonight."

"Unfortunate," Keith said, spreading his hands. "Things don't always work out. But what I can assure you is this: You don't do as I like, it won't work out for you, and Hap here...I assume that's who you are. Alton described you. Said you were like a once nice-looking guy who had gone through a wringer and then been heated up in a microwave."

"Now I'm glad I shot him," I said.

I was talking to Keith, but I watched the woman in the back, making sure Keith's conversation wasn't just misdirection. That plasti-glass could take a solid hit, but still, I watched her. My take was, she made a move, I was going to shoot through the speaker hole and blow a canyon in Keith's chest. He was lined up good for that.

"Just so you know, you're thinking about shooting me through that little hole, you would have to be quick."

The son of a bitch read my mind.

"And then I got a vest on. Good one. Better than the ones you two are wearing, I assure you. And that locked door? Once shots are fired, my crew will come inside. Door being locked won't matter. It'll be as easy as throwing rocks through cotton candy. And that plastic in front of you, it's tough, but we got weapons that will make it seem like nothing."

"You don't have a vest on your head," I said.

"You'd have to be a really good shot, restrictions of that

hole and all. And if you hit that little metal framing, who knows where a bullet could go?"

"Look, you got something to say, say it," Manny said. "I'm starting to get bored."

I sneaked a glance at my watch. The time was being eaten up, and if Leonard left when we agreed he should leave, I wanted us to be on that bus. All Manny and I were doing was stalling to make sure the noncombatants got on.

It wouldn't be too long before Jordan hit the switch in the generator room and all the lights went out. That would be our cue to haul ass.

Manny sighed, said, "Why don't you give us the short-story version of whatever novel you got in mind to tell us, whatever you got in mind to stall us with while you do whatever you think is going to work."

"As if I don't think you got some kind of plan going," Keith said.

Manny said nothing.

Keith leaned back in the chair. He looked comfortable. I half expected him to put on pajamas.

"Very well," he said. "Let me lay it out for you."

"Lay what out?" Manny said.

"What you're going to end up doing."

34

Standing in that reception room thinking on it, waiting for those lights to go off, suddenly our little plan seemed goddamn crazy. We would have a long way to haul with people on our ass, and Wilson Keith, he was smooth and deadly and had the soul of a piranha but with less compassion.

And if we made it to the bus, Leonard had to drive it through the locked gate, and after that, well . . . I didn't know. I didn't know pig shit from axle grease. It was all a big crapshoot, and Keith had the loaded dice, not us. What we had was a wish and a hope and an old transport bus.

But Leonard was out there waiting. That was something. Still, bad as it looked for me and Manny, I hoped he wouldn't wait too long if we were delayed. I wanted to know he and the others, that little girl Nikki, got out of there alive and well.

I could feel my palm sweating on the back of the chair I was touching. Keith's voice seemed to be an echo. I took a deep breath, used my martial arts training to find my center. It was dark at that center, and a little loud from the thumping of my heart, but I found it, and I began to relax.

Keith had never stopped talking.

"...have to do is consider the reality of your situation. Reality is what dictates ethics and decisions, not morality. Something is fine and moral and ethical until it's about you and your life. We can all afford to be ethical and moral when our lives don't matter, but in this case, frankly, yours matters a lot."

"Situational ethics," Manny said.

"That's one way to put it, but I call it realism," Keith said. "You can do nice and fine and right when your ass isn't on the line, but when it's money or sex or your life, a person's viewpoint changes. Let me tell you what you should already know. You're old enough to have left your teddy bears behind. The world isn't fair, and right now, you're caught in the unfair part. Idealism is a shield that melts with age and experience. You must know that. You must know you're holding only a piece of that shield now, or maybe you know it's gone already, but, out of habit, you keep hanging on to that bullshit we were all taught when we were young. Think about it. Everyone's dipping their snouts in the trough. What I'm doing is cutting right through the shit. I don't know you. I wouldn't care if I did. I neither like nor dislike you, but to suit myself, to put things at an easier advantage for me, I'm willing to do for you what lobbyists do for politicians. I'm going to offer you money, and you can be my little representatives. Hell, I'll promote you to senators."

"I have a feeling we might end up like the jailer your son hired, under some tin at a junkyard dump," I said.

"He took the money, but he didn't live up to his end of the bargain. My son picked the kind of guy that was a little too proud of himself and couldn't keep his mouth shut."

"But us, who you've known a few minutes, we're a wise pick?" Manny said.

"I'm picking you, my son isn't. He couldn't pick a rotten cucumber over a ripe one. And just for the record, Alton was on my payroll for some time. Let me add something else while we're having this discussion. Little Miss Nicole has false recollections."

"Could be," I said. "But I think she's closer to the truth than you are. Her tongue is a lot better now. I thought she talked quite convincingly, although I had to listen close. She's already got a written statement in, so even if something happened to her, shit, man, you're sunk."

"In the end, it's her word against mine. And I have a few of my spots picked, so to speak."

"Spots?" I said.

"He means money invested in lawmakers," Manny said. "More crooked cops like Alton."

"You said that, not me. I only hinted that I have friends in high places. Cops are actually on the bottom of the stack. There are others I have in my pockets, and they have more power. I'm merely suggesting we should be friends because it would be in your best interests."

"We are not your friends," Manny said.

"You ought to try to be."

"I was a friend of yours, even a passing acquaintance, I wouldn't like to look at myself in the mirror, see what was in it," I said. "Besides, you just made it perfectly clear no one is worthy of having a friend, because in the end, we're all going to turn on one another if the need arises."

"Mr. Collins, you are just a half-assed private investigator. Surely you see and do some pretty unworthy things from time to time."

"There are lines I don't cross."

"Let me put this in a way that will make sense to both of you. We all have loved ones. Some of them, like my son, who is outside, can be a cross to bear. There are times I think a sack of shit and the brain in that boy's head couldn't be any different, but he is my son. That said, if it comes down to me or him, I'll tell you truly, and I don't know that he knows this, but considering how I've lived my life, he must have some idea ... I would throw his ass under the bus, and I would drive the bus over him, then back it up if it was about my survival. My dick still works, and I can find a woman to bear a child. I can make another son, but the empire I've put together, I can't remake so easily. You two, however, being as you're such idealists, might be more considerate of your family, and therefore maybe you truly would try to jump in front of the bus I'm driving to protect them. You do, that bus will run right over you. But if you want to get on the bus, well, hey, I can make room for both of you, and your friends and family too. Hell, bring the dog and cat, a pet goat, I don't give a shit. But it has to come out my way."

I saw where he was going with this. I hoped Brett had decided to leave, to go on to Tyler and take everyone with her. I wished I had been able to call her and verify that. I wished a lot of things right then. I took a deep breath, tried not to show how scared I was. I put a smile on my face. Maybe Keith was right. Maybe it all did come down to situational ethics.

"You didn't put together shit," I said. "You took over this crew and all the money that came with it when the people who had it before got nabbed, killed, or you helped finish them off. You didn't build a goddamn thing. You took in a short time what others spent years building. Not that I have any admiration for those assholes either."

"The ability to take something is important, Mr. Collins. That's called having the wisdom to recognize favorable circumstances. It's called power."

"Is that what it is?" I said.

"I'm giving you both an opportunity. I don't know where Mr. Pine is, but I am giving him the same opportunity. I want it to go well for all of you and the people close to you. That said, you make a different choice, I got to do what I got to do. I mean, hell, I know who you two are, and I know who matters to you."

"Let me give you a note, and you might want to stick this

on your refrigerator. My family, you touch them, and I will kill you and everyone who works for you."

He laughed. "That's bold for a fifty-year-old man."

"I'll help him," Manny said. "And let me tell you something. Hap, he's spry."

"This is your one chance to walk out of here instead of what's left of you being washed out with a hose. Let us have Miss Beckman. You don't even know her. She's just a chink white-trash bitch, and I do mean white, who stuck her nose in where she shouldn't have. You want to give up your life for someone you don't know? You don't even have to hand her over, so you won't have that on your conscience. Just leave, and we'll take care of her. You'll find a nice package in the mail in a few days, something substantial inside that will help you forget what happened here . . . You can say we took you by surprise, put you in a jail cell, then grabbed the girl. We could do that, you know. Put you in a cell so it doesn't look too obvious. There are ways to make this look okay."

"You're not letting us walk," I said. "You're not letting anyone walk. And I couldn't forget doing something like that if I got a million-dollar check weekly and starlets from Hollywood came in daily to hold my balls while I changed pants. I'd rather be dead. Though the starlets would be nice."

"You realize I'm suggesting it could turn out that way, Mr. Collins. Not the starlets. The dead part."

"In the long run, the law will get you," Manny said.

"That is so precious. I keep telling you, the law and justice and the American way goes out the window when money shows up."

"Not for everyone," Manny said.

"People love the power of the law, not the law. Christians don't love Jesus, they love John Wayne. Kindness to the poor and the meek, do you see that happening? Turn the other cheek? And another thing—I can't let small-time assholes like this girl run over me and my family business. I let this go, then others will challenge me. Maybe those others will be a lot better than you two and some split-tail albino. You have to have some standards, you're going to run a business, especially my kind of business."

I glanced at my hand resting on the back of the chair, at my watch. It was just about that time.

If Jordan didn't fuck it up.

"We might be better than you think," I said.

"And you might not," Keith said.

"Listen," I said. "Let me ask you a question. Do you ever wonder what it's like when it goes completely dark?"

"What?" he said.

The generator lights went out.

35

Dead black.

Jordan had done his job, and on time. It was so dark you couldn't see an inch in front of you.

I heard Manny slip out of the chair, and then me and her started for the door, making our way by memory and feel. Shots were blindly fired. I could hear them hit the plasti-glass, but that stubborn stuff held, though it wouldn't for long.

Manny and I ran for it. I tried to charge through the doorway at the back and ran smack into the wall.

I heard Manny fall; I groped around for her, got her up. I reached in my pocket for the flashlight, brought it out, popped it on. We could see the open doorway and went through it. Behind us I heard the plasti-glass crack from more gunfire.

When we were through the door I made sure it was closed

tight, put the chair under it, but Manny had a better idea. In the glow of my flashlight, she used the keypad by the door to lock it, then we grabbed up the guns and slickers and hustled toward the exit.

We got to where we could see the door that led to the generator. It was wide open. The flashlight showed no one was in there. Jordan had hauled ass like he was supposed to.

We moved to the other open doorway, one that led into the short hall that extended to the exit. We hurried along, and as we got closer to the end of the hallway, I turned off the flashlight, jammed it in my pocket.

We hit the exit door like a stampeding buffalo herd, and all of a sudden, we were outside in the coal-mine dark, the rain slashing us, the wind blowing our hair, cutting us like cold razor blades. It was so dark we couldn't see the steps under us. We couldn't see the bus. Hell, we couldn't see the parking lot.

"We'll have to use a light," Manny said.

I fumbled my long gun to her, and against my better judgment, I got out the flashlight. I turned it on, flicked the light toward the lot so we could see the bus. I got a glimpse of Leonard at the wheel, other shapes behind the wire-net-and-glass windows, and then we were moving swiftly, slipping a little as we went. Water was not so deep there, but it was deep enough to flow over our ankles. It was cold, and it took only a few steps before you could feel it seep into the flesh and chill your bones. It was so unsettling and uncomfortable, I think a polar bear would have taken his chances back inside the cop shop.

"I'm cutting the light," I said, "keep going straight."

I cut it. We kept plowing ahead. And then there was a shot.
It zipped through the night and slammed into something, but
thankfully that something wasn't us. Next thing we knew, we
were running up against the bus, feeling our way around it,
making our way to the door. I could hear the bus motor hum-
ming, and then I heard the hydraulic door open. There was a
dull green light on the dash of the bus, and that made it so we
could see. Leonard's face was softly painted by the light. He
smiled green teeth at me.

"Good to see you," he said.

"Likewise." I glanced toward the back of the bus. Shapes.
Except for Nikki—she was closer to the front—I couldn't
make out anyone.

"Everyone good?" I said.

Everyone agreed they felt good enough, then Jordan said,
"Come on, man, let's go."

Me and Manny took seats, she behind Leonard, me on the
right side not too far from the door. The door hissed closed.

"Grab your asses," Leonard said. "Here goes."

With that, he shifted a gear, the bus jumped a little, and
away we went, straight for the locked fence gate.

36

Shots were hitting the bus now.

"This thing is reasonably bulletproof," Manny said. "Tires are designed to take small-arms fire. It's built like a tank."

"Let's hope so," Leonard said, then he stomped the gas.

We hit the gate, and *bam,* I was nearly jolted to the front of the bus, and then I was thrown out of the seat and onto the floor. I hustled myself back into place.

The gate was knocked flat, and we rattled over it, rolling toward what looked like too much water.

Leonard turned right and climbed the hill toward North Street, away from the deep stuff, but water was running down the hill in a silver shine and splashing along the sides of the bus. Leonard turned the headlights on.

In the headlights, the rain on the road looked slick and snotty. It came down fast and looked like a beaded curtain.

We were near the top of the hill when the dump truck Leonard told us about charged out of the alley, its headlights off. It hit the right side of the bus with a sound like the crack of doom.

I heard people flying around in the back of the bus, and I was thrown across the aisle and splayed over the seat where Manny had been sitting and was now lying.

"Goddamn, Hap, get off me," she said.

The bus didn't spin, it just slid on a coating of water. The dump truck kept pushing. Soon we'd be across the street and smacked up against a building.

I grabbed the pole that was near the front of the bus, used it to guide myself back into my seat again, all of this performed as we slid in slow motion, pushed by that dump truck, its tires struggling to maintain traction.

Leonard jerked the wheel to the left, right toward where I feared we would collide, and gave it the gas. The front of the bus went left, and the back of it spun right. The back end of the bus hit the dump truck and made it slide, turned it so that it was facing the way it had come.

"Damn, you do that on purpose?" I said.

"Of course," he said.

I could tell he was lying.

Leonard turned the bus around as adroitly as a professional stunt-car driver, and that was probably an accident too. He drove the bus left through an alleyway, and it looked like a clean escape, and then, damn, that garbage truck Leonard said had been parked out front of the cop shop with the dump truck was at the end of the alley, shiny white in the bus headlights. I could see that big killer I had shot in the hospital sitting behind the wheel. The way the lights hit him, he looked like an obsidian golem. Keith and his minions had planned ahead, moved the garbage and dump trucks into position to block the exits.

We were speeding toward a head-on collision.

Leonard slammed on the brakes. The bus slipped a little, made us feel like it was on wet grass. And then he was in reverse, gunning it back out of the alley, using the side mirror to plan his path. A precarious thing, since most of what he had for lighting were the now-busted backup lights. The garbage truck's lights came on, and the truck roared and rattled after us.

"We're all going to die," the female dispatcher said.

"Possible," I heard Manny say.

37

The lights from the garbage truck filled the bus like watery honey. I sat looking backward, the direction we were going. In the lights from the garbage truck, I could see the dispatchers clinging to the backs of the seats in front of them. Someone was praying. The others were cursing. Nikki was quiet, something not so surprising for a lady with a sore tongue. Manny and I joined her in silence. Leonard, inexplicably, had started singing "Mama's Little Baby Loves Short'nin' Bread."

If that wasn't bad enough, the dump truck was back in the game, and it had turned on its lights and was driving for us, trying to sandwich us between several tons of speeding metal. I was already imagining them finding me with a transmission up my ass, my teeth full of the windshield.

But Leonard had a bit of a lead on them, and he made it

out of the alley before the dump truck hit our ass, before the garbage truck plowed our front.

He whipped the bus toward the hill that rose up to North Street and gave it the gas. It got traction easier than expected and started climbing. The dump truck looked certain to clip our ass, but it just missed.

Unfortunately for the dump-truck driver, he couldn't slow in time to avoid the garbage truck. I looked behind me and saw them ram together, maybe six inches from the back of our ride. It was a hell of a smack and you could hear the brakes grinding on both trucks as they tried unsuccessfully to prevent a collision.

In the bus taillights, I saw the passenger door on the dump truck spring open, and then I caught the driver's circus act as he was thrown out of the truck by the impact, into the wet street.

I blinked in amazement when he rolled and came up on his feet. It was that little kung fu fucker we had fought in the hospital. He looked devilish in the taillights. I had done martial arts all my life, and I didn't think people like that were for real, just in the movies.

He shot us the finger as we roared away and he disappeared into darkness behind us.

Same to you, I thought.

Leonard was no longer singing. He was whistling the shortening-bread tune.

On up the road we rolled, and then we were on North Street. We turned left, went two streets down, and turned right.

"Where're you going?" Manny said.

"Where am I supposed to be going?"

"Tyler, that's where we need to go now."

"I think I'm going to Hap's house."

"You're out of your mind."

Leonard turned his head sharply, looked at me. "Am I out of my mind, Hap?"

"No, sir, that's exactly where you need to go. I need to be sure they got out."

"Oh," Manny said. "Of course. I don't have a family. Even my dog died."

The bus went along that way and we passed some houses, and then we turned right, hoping we could get back to my place.

We made it all right for a while, and then it was obvious we couldn't continue, not in that bus, not the way we were going. We came to where a house had been destroyed and the wind and rain had pushed much of it into the street. To turn right was to drive into a vast pool of water and risk being stuck, and to go left meant we would be blocked by trees and lumber.

"Goddamn it," I said.

Leonard backed the bus into a driveway, turned it around without letting it slip too far into where water had gathered in an incline, and drove back the way we had come. He turned right, hit University, turned left on it. The road was open where it had been closed to us before, and where it had been open to us, now there were trees

191

and cars and wooden debris. The water park and its water slides were gone.

Leonard made a few false starts, took a variety of roads, wove the bus through all manner of messes, ran over people's yards where they were clear, and finally made it to my place.

When we got there, Leonard sprang the door open, and I leaped out and ran toward the dark house. As I neared, using my flashlight, I noted that most of the roof was gone and a tree from somewhere, a large tree, had gone through the right side of the house like a spear.

I was going to use my key, but the door wasn't locked. I went in fast, the flashlight in my left hand, my right holding the pistol.

I called everyone's name, including Buffy's.

No one came.

I ran up the stairs with the light bobbing in front of me, and when I got to the top I pushed into our bedroom. The bed had collapsed under some fallen roof timbers, and the room was wet and smelled bad. I could see the dark sky through the hole in the roof and I could hear the wind and the rain. The world had gone to hell in a wet handbasket.

I checked the other rooms upstairs. They were intact. I went downstairs, shone the light around, saw the kitchen window had been knocked out by something. Air whistled through it like wind in a cave. It was then that I saw there was a note on the table, held down by a salt shaker.

I put the flashlight on it.

It said: *You know where, baby. Love, Brett*

I did know where. The first hotel or motel in Tyler that took dogs and was near the mall and Half Price Books. They had slipped away in time. I breathed a sigh of relief, shivered, and then I was okay. I went out to the bus.

38

We passed the one and only real hotel in LaBorde, saw there were some dim lights inside, most likely from a weak generator. Leonard pulled over there. We let out the dispatchers and the nurse. Manny and I got off with them, went inside, leaving Leonard at the wheel and Nikki still in her seat.

We weren't letting her out of our sight.

We found a clerk sitting behind a desk. The only light there was a small lamp on the side of the long desk. The nurse and the dispatchers bunched up close to us. Our shoes made little puddles and mud marks on the tile.

"Bad night," said the clerk. He was a young black man

with a tight haircut, a tight necktie, and a condom-tight suit. He looked a little excited in the lamplight.

"Police," Manny said, and pulled out her badge. She gave the clerk some info, but didn't give him all the juice. The clerk explained they only had an old backup generator working. The facilities were inadequate. No elevator. No lights in the hallway. Limited light in the rooms. No room service, as if he thought we might be planning to order coffee and pie.

"It'll do," Manny said. "Bill the department."

We spoke in a comforting manner to the dispatchers and the nurse, told them to sit tight until they got word to leave.

The clerk started sorting out room keys.

"We should go," Manny said.

"Good luck," the female dispatcher said.

"Yeah," Jordan said. "Good luck."

"You done good with that generator," I said.

"I just flicked a switch."

"Still," I said, "you done good."

"I really should stay with you," the nurse said. "The girl is my patient."

"I don't think that's best," Manny said. "We'll take care of her."

The nurse hesitated. I could tell she was torn between duty and common sense. "Here," the nurse said, opened her purse and gave me a couple bottles of pills. "I brought these with me. She needs this one about every four hours. The other, well, twice a day."

I took the pills and slipped them in my windbreaker pocket.

Manny said to the clerk, "Hey, you got a hotel van?"

"We do," the clerk said.

"You better put that on the bill too."

39

Nikki and I rode together in the courtesy van from the hotel, following the big white bus with Leonard and Manny on it.

"What are we doing?" Nikki said.

It surprised me when she spoke. She hadn't in a while. "We're going to ditch the bus, which is what they're looking for, try to get you to Tyler, to the cops there, some medical attention."

"Will that be any safer?"

"We'll be with you," I said.

"He may have paid someone off. That's what the Keiths do."

"Not all cops are like that."

"Only takes one."

"We're going to see that you're protected. Manny will be there too. You're her duty, and we're making you ours."

"I am such an idiot. I believed Pretty Boy, and I should have known better. No. That's a lie. I did know better. I wanted some adventure, a bad boy. Was that stupid?"

"Yes."

She made a kind of snicker sound. "Yeah. It was. What's with women and bad boys?"

"I have no idea. What is with them?"

"I had such a strange growing-up. My parents, they were fine, but me being albino, kids at school, they didn't know what to do with that. And there have been some health issues, and there was no sunbathing or swimming during the day, and during the summer I didn't go to camp . . . is this starting to sound like a poor-me rant?"

"A little."

"Yeah, I know. Everyone has a story."

"Where you are now is due to bad choices, Nikki, but it's not your fault that Pretty Boy turned out to be a big shit and a coward. I got a list of bad choices, girl. I have a lot of blood on my hands."

"Some of it was for me."

"A lot of it is for other reasons. I'm all the things I never meant to be. You got a chance now to move on, to get in a better groove. This is your break."

"You bet I'm going to try. But Keith—all the energy and resources being put out to kill me, doesn't make sense. I've already given enough evidence to get them in trouble even if I am killed. What's the point?"

"It's not all about you," I said. "It's about Keith's pride, about who's the big boss, and with the weather like it is, I think he feels more powerful, a real renegade. It's like the apocalypse, and it's everyone for themselves. Thing is, though, he's scared."

"Scared?"

"His big show of power is about hanging on to the spot he's got. Had his druthers, LaBorde would look like Juarez at the height of the drug war. Kind of guy that would decapitate folks and hang bodies off bridges and from trees. Knew some of the guys in the Dixie Mafia before him. They were trouble too. But they were mostly low-profile. It's Keith's posturing that will do him in. Or he'll run up against someone he can't handle."

"I hope so," she said. "I better be quiet. My tongue is swelling."

I drove with one hand and used the other to fish out one of her bottles of pills. "Can you swallow like a chicken, without water?"

"Yeah."

I gave her the bottle. "One pill," I said.

She took one out and gave me the bottle back. I put it back in my slicker pocket.

"I can't explain to you how grateful I am to you and Leonard. That's right, isn't it? Leonard. Manny told me, but I'm not sure I remember it right."

"Yeah, and just in case you don't know for sure, when it comes to me, I'm Hap."

"You didn't have to help me."

"Yes, we did."

Ahead of us, Leonard turned up a big hill with dark apartments perched on it, drove around a curve and then along a wooded road that was right in the middle of LaBorde. It looked like a country lane.

He pulled over to the side of the road and parked the bus so it was leaning toward a ditch.

He and Manny got out on the ditch side without falling into it, eased their way to us, and climbed into the van.

"Take us to Tyler," Leonard said. "And don't spare the horses."

"Yes, boss," I said.

40

It seemed simple enough, and I was starting to feel encouraged. All we had to do was drive to Tyler. Keith and his men weren't looking for a white van. We had already reached North Street again, and the path was clear enough to navigate. There were few lights on along the street, and everything was quiet and still. No other cars were on the road.

I checked the rearview mirror. Nope. No one was following us.

We rode on out until we were at the end of LaBorde, near where the old abandoned LaBorde Bowling Center was. We passed it and drove up a rise in the highway and came down on the other side, and there was a disaster.

There had been a bad pileup of trucks and there was a dead cow in the road. Trees that must have been two hundred years old had been uprooted by the wind and the rain and thrown into the pile of dead bovine and twisted metal.

We parked the van, and me and Leonard got out in the rain, left Manny with Nikki. The rain had slowed and the wind was mild for a change, but we still weren't much encouraged. We walked around and looked in the trucks, poking around with my flashlight, but there was no one there. It was obvious this had all happened some time back, maybe yesterday afternoon or last night, and whoever had been here had either walked off or been taken by ambulance to the hospital. At this point, there were probably no ambulances running, or they were running in a limited way. There was no way to call a wrecker to have this stuff moved. No way to do much of anything. And as far as the police went, well, the entirety of the available Laborde Police Department was behind us in a van.

I felt odd right then, how prehistoric man must have felt when the night came and storms stirred up. The edge of the road was mostly forest, but it looked like a black wall, except at the top where the trees sighed in the wind and the sky was a little fainter, but if the rain came back and the wind picked up, then it would be solid black up there too, like being inside a bag of shadows.

"You okay?" Leonard said.

"No."

"Me either."

"The bowling center," I said.

"What?"

"We hole up there, park the van around back, wait until daybreak. Maybe the repair crews will open up the road, some cops can come into work."

"In the old science fiction movies, they always called in the National Guard or the army."

"That'll work too," I said.

"You know, it might even be the best plan. I don't know about you, but I feel like I was whupped with a knotted plow line, buried in a bucket of shit, and brought back to life with a shot of electricity. I got the coffee jitters but at the same time I feel like I could lie down on broken glass and sleep."

"Yeah. I'm getting a little weak, not to mention hungry."

"Me too. My stomach thinks my throat's cut."

We went back to the van and told Manny our plan, which she eagerly agreed to. Truth was, we were all starting to slow down as the fear and excitement wore off. We drove back to the bowling center and parked behind it.

It was huge. There had not only been a bowling alley there but also a place for games, and there had been upstairs apartments where the owners lived.

The back door was locked, of course, and neither Leonard nor I had our lock picks with us. We had misplaced them along the way.

"Shall we kick it in?" Manny said.

I got a straight tire iron out of the back of the van and went over and stuck it into the edge of the door, worked it a little, and popped the door loose. Everyone but me went inside. I went back to the van and pulled it up against the door sideways, so I could open the door, squeeze a bit, and step into the bowling alley. When I was inside, I closed the van door and then the bowling-alley door and hoped the van door would be a bit of a barrier if it came down to it.

Right then, though, I felt snug and safe and thought it was highly unlikely Keith and his minions would find us. I felt that by that point, we'd shaken them.

Manny was bouncing her flashlight beam around the bowling alley, and the place was massive. I got my own light out, started moving it about. The bowling alley had been closed for at least ten years, and for a couple of years, there was talk that it would be reopened. A For Sale sign went up, but no one bit. There was a rumor that a fellow was going to buy it and turn it into a skating rink, but that never happened. The potential buyer probably decided if people didn't come to bowl, they wouldn't come to skate.

The air had been stirred by our arrival, and in the beam of the flashlights we could see dust moving, and the wood lanes were a muted gold, and the balls in the racks at the head of the alleys looked like little boulders.

I shone my light down one of the lanes, and I could see some bowling pins turned over inside the open troughs where the balls fell through. The pin rack was halfway down, but it hadn't picked up any pins, and I could almost hear bowling balls smacking them, like the story of Rip Van Winkle, where he discovered the old men in the mountains playing ninepins.

In the other direction, there was a long row of seats in front of the alleys, and there were a dozen alleys, and there were honey-colored couches where you could recline while waiting your turn to bowl. Behind those was a short wall, and you could see over that to a long rack of small shelves where you picked up bowling shoes. There were still shoes in those shelves, covered in dust and linked by cobwebs. There was a stairway next to the rack that led to the second floor.

I flashed my light on the stairway that went up, then turned left and out of sight behind a wall. There was a long row of windows above the stairs, and it was broken up by some wood frames at eight-foot intervals all the way across, and it was like that over the shoe counter and all along the top of the bowling alley, and the windows ran on two sides. That way the managers could be upstairs and look down on the alley through the long row of windows and make sure no one was walking off with bowling shoes or a bowling ball while they had gone upstairs to grab a sandwich or use the toilet.

Leonard came out of a doorless room next to the pin racks with his cell phone light on.

We all went in there for a look, and there were still snacks inside the machines. Leonard used his windbreaker sleeve to wipe the dust off the glass of the closest machine so we could see inside more clearly.

"Jesus," Manny said, "that stuff is as old as Methuselah's grandpa."

"I was hoping for a Twinkie," Leonard said. "They say those last forever, all the preservatives in them. I'm about ready to look for mice to eat."

"That you could probably find," Manny said, "and fresh, but

that stuff in the machines, I wouldn't suggest trying it, otherwise you might end up blowing out your bowels."

With food out of the picture, we went upstairs and moved the lights around. It was spacious up there, and there were several rooms, and there was a toilet, but it didn't have any water connected to it, so that wasn't going to be a plus, and worse yet, just seeing it made me want to pee or take a dump.

After looking in all the rooms, we went down and gravitated without a word toward the couches. We laid our long guns on the floor in front of them.

Nikki stretched out on one of the couches, and when she did, the dust from it stirred up and spun in my flashlight beam. Manny stretched out on another, and me and Leonard sat for a bit, and then suddenly I felt all fired up again, got up, and went to where I could walk behind the lanes and look at the racks for the bowling pins. Leonard came with me. We are adventurers.

"You thinking about trying a vending-machine snack anyway," he said.

"Too much work to break into one," I said. "And I'm not so hungry I'm willing to chance it."

"Yep. You know, I bowled here a couple of times. Did you know this is where you could meet men if you were gay?"

"I bet it's where heterosexuals could meet folks too," I said.

"You know, you're probably right. Sometimes I wish life were simple like back then."

"You mean when you had separate water fountains and toilets?"

"No. After that. When I could come here."

"I'm not so sure those days were the sweet spot we make them in memory."

"You might be right," Leonard said.

We got bored and tired all over again, and we bold adventurers went back to the spare couches, chose one apiece, stretched out. I was asleep so fast, I don't really remember putting my head against the dusty backrest of the couch.

41

I wasn't out long before the wind woke me up. The rain was coming down hard again too. I could hear it running through the roof somewhere, dripping into the bowling alley.

I had gone from a dead sleep to being wide awake, and right now that wind and that rain seemed to be the only sounds in the world. I got up with my light and discovered that near the wide front doors, just over them on the inside, there was a leak. The ceiling had been taking a weather beating for a long time, and the rain was slipping in and running onto the floor, and the floor had warped slightly and that part of the place smelled of mildew and what I assumed from experience was rat turds.

I hadn't seen that leak when I was on the second floor. That seemed real important to me right then, like maybe I was surveying property I intended to buy. I guessed it had

been leaking through the roof above the shower and drain-
ing along the edges of the shower, breaking open the ceiling
over time. A few more years and that whole section would
come down.

I thought I should try to go back to sleep, but then I
heard something outside that wasn't the wind and the rain
but a loud growling sound. I went to the wire-mesh window on one side of the door and looked out. There was a
row of lights on top of something moving toward the bowling center.

It was coming up the long drive toward the bowling alley,
splashing through the rain. I could tell the way the lights were
set and the way it moved that it was the vehicle Leonard had
described after looking out the front door of the cop shop. It
came to a stop about fifty feet from the front door.

But how had they found us?

"Hey," I called out as I turned off my flashlight. "The assholes are here."

It took me a couple of calls to wake Manny and Leonard
up, but when they were awake, they got their long guns
and came over and stood near me and looked out the
window.

Nikki didn't have a gun, but she came over too. I was glad I
had forgotten to give her one of those pills that would knock
her out. It was best we were all alert now.

"How the hell?" Leonard said.

And then the walkie clipped to Manny's belt squawked.

"Ah, shit," Manny said.

She pulled the walkie off her belt, touched a button, and a voice said, "You know, I have a tracker in the walkie-talkies to make sure I have all my men in place. I got the gear to track you without having to do anything other than climb inside my truck. This thing has a nice movie screen, impossibly comfortable seats, a winch, this bullhorn, and the nice spotlights you are currently experiencing. It even has a wet bar. Fact is, right now I'm sipping a glass of premium scotch. Anyway, I know you're in there. Look, send snow girl out, and we'll make it quick for her, and the rest of you, we let you go."

Manny clicked the walkie. "We been through this."

"Yeah," said Keith's voice. "I know you know I'm bullshitting you, but I wanted to see what would happen. I thought maybe you had turned stupid."

"Look, we're going to be generous," Manny said. "If you surrender to us now, no one gets hurt."

We could hear Keith laugh.

Manny dropped the walkie-talkie on the floor and put her foot on it and it snapped into pieces.

"Sort of figured he wasn't going to surrender," she said.

Now came a loudspeaker voice from a device attached to the security vehicle. It was louder than the walkie-talkie, and it was Keith laughing at us. He didn't say a word, just laughed like an idiot, and then there was silence.

"Seen too many James Bond films," Leonard said.

While we watched through the long glass window, the door to the vehicle opened on the right side, and a big man got out. He was the big black man who had been driving the garbage truck. He had a long gun of some sort. He was the man I had shot. He was a black Hulk. All he needed to do then was say "Me smash."

A moment later an SUV pulled up behind the security vehicle and five shapes got out of it. I couldn't make out any of them, really.

"See Kung Fu Bobby out there?" Leonard said.

"There's one guy smaller than the others, I think that's him."

"Yeah, could be," Leonard said. "What is that motherfucker, a cat? Ought to be in some kind of circus act or trying out for the Olympics or something."

"Maybe you can rep him?"

"Think I could make him and me a lot of money."

I saw the big black man raise his weapon. "Quick," I said. "Step away."

And step we did. The glass beside the door burst apart and the wire woven inside the glass was twisted. The bullet smacked something in the background but, fortunately, none of us.

We hurried to the couches. I'm not sure why, but it had suddenly become our gathering point.

I said, "They'll be coming in, and pretty quick. Maybe the front door, maybe the back, probably both. They'll hook the winch on that truck out there to the van and pull it away. It'll be easy."

"Upstairs," Manny said.

"I don't love that idea," Leonard said.

"Until you got a better one, I'm taking Nikki up there with me. I might be able to hold them off better from that position."

"Oh God," Nikki said.

"I'm going to do my best to protect you," Manny said.

"Her best is damn good," I said.

Nikki nodded, but she was beginning to tremble.

Manny headed for the stairs, Nikki following, Leonard and me pulling up the rear. When we got to where the stairs turned, me and Leonard stopped. I said, "I'll stay here at the corner, see if I can hold them a bit. Maybe you can find a way out up there."

"Yeah, we'll just turn ourselves to water and slip down the drain. Shit, Hap, we get up there, we might as well bend over and kiss our asses good-bye. Or there's always the roof. We might find a hole somewhere leads up there, but then they can climb up and shoot at us until they hit something."

"I'm sorry to say I'm not exactly full of fresh ideas."

"I got one," Leonard said. "You stay here, and I'll go down and get behind the pin racks, take a position in an opening. They might not expect that, and it'll give me some cover."

"You know I should do that, not you."

"Why is that?"

"Because you can't shoot like me. I need to catch the first ones in."

Leonard sighed.

"Shit, you're probably right. Hate it when you're right. I'll stay here at the stairs, maybe we can get them in a cross fire or some such."

"Just don't get me in that cross fire. I'll be the handsome white man hiding in one of the pin openings. I want to stay handsome and alive."

"You ain't handsome."

"Then let's just make sure I stay alive."

Manny came back down the stairs. "What the hell, boys?"

I told her.

She gave Leonard her long gun. "You'll need this, and I'll take your handgun to add to mine, maybe give one to Nikki. It might come to that."

Leonard gave it to her. I reached for my handgun.

"Keep it," Manny said. "I think you might need a lot of ammunition." She gave me some of her ammunition to go with the long gun, and Leonard gave me some of his; all the sets matched. I had automatic rifles and a shotgun and a pistol now. If I only had crossing bandoliers.

"I'll try to barricade upstairs, protect Nikki," Manny said. "But that will leave you out here, Leonard."

"I'd rather be where I can see Hap."

"All right."

"If you can get out with Nikki, get out," I said.

"Believe me, I'd have no trouble leaving your asses behind, but I'm not sure there's a way out. Nice knowing you boys."

"Same to you," I said.

Manny went back up and I slipped down the stairs and skulked to one of the wooden lanes and went down it with my body bent. I slid in on my side where a bowling-pin drop was open, wiggled on through.

When I was in the path behind where the pins were racked, I tracked along the openings back there, found one I thought best, one where I could see the front door. They came through the back door, they had to come along the side of the alley, and since I was in the center, eventually I would see them as they came forward. And Leonard would have them right in line for a shot.

I looked and saw Leonard's shadow at the place where the stairs turned, and then his shadow slipped out of view behind the wall. I took a deep breath to calm my nerves a little, but it was the kind of calm that wouldn't last, and the air tasted like the dust from a mummy's shroud.

The truck lights went away and left the windows at the front of the bowling center dark, and then I heard that big damn truck rolling along the side of the building, and then it was at the back. A 747 could have landed with less noise than that mechanical beast.

And then I heard the sound of the winch out back being snapped into place, and then I heard it pulling the van away from the door, as I suspected they would do, and then the front door cracked and turned my attention there as wind and rain spilled into the room.

Someone was trying to be clever and push it open in the dark slowly, but I saw it.

I saw it all right.

But nothing happened, not right away. Damn, they were

coming from both ends of the building, and soon the place would be swarming with them.

I took a deep breath, told myself, "I still live," using the mantra of one of my favorite childhood fictional heroes, John Carter of Mars.

42

———

Things began to slow and I felt fear crawling along my spine like a centipede. I was tired and I was dealing with a lot of assholes, and I wasn't sure I could handle it from all angles, even if I had a fair view of everything. I placed the gun on the alley beneath the pin rack and waited. My hands were sweating and I felt warm, even though the air wasn't all that humid.

In fact, the front door was wide open now, and the wind and rain were coming inside, and it was a cool wind, I guess, but I sure wasn't cool. My blood was boiling with fearful anticipation. I thought: I have killed before, and I can do it again, and maybe I can do it too easily. All these goddamn guns, and all these bad places I put myself into, and no matter how I justified it, I was a goddamn killer. I had crossed the line a long time ago, and you can't uncross that line, and that's what's scary.

I wiped my damp hands on my pants, picked up the long gun.

I saw a shadow slip through the door, a shadow with an automatic rifle, I presumed. I had him in my sight, and I eased the trigger slowly as I gently let out my breath. I can't describe why I can shoot like I can, but I've always had the knack. I learned early on how to shoot, but there was nothing classical about it. I didn't really care for guns at all, but if you put one in my hand, it was like a natural extension. Where I pointed, I could quite often hit, and right then I was pointing at that shadow, and as my breath was eased and the trigger was pulled, I saw the top of the shadow, where the head was, become a black swarm like bees flying out from their hive. The shape collapsed in a heap to the floor and the shadowy swarm splattered against the wall.

And then the back door was slung open, and though I couldn't quite see it, I could hear them coming through. Three or four steps in, they would be visible if I angled myself a little, but now others were coming through the front door, and they were firing in my direction. I wasn't sure if they saw me or had seen the gunfire, but now I held the trigger down and let the sparks fly, filling that doorway with hot destruction.

I figured they had a plan to get me busy on one end, then take me from the other, but I knew Leonard was facing the back door from the stairwell, so I decided to forget about the back door, concentrate on the front.

There was fire from the stairway toward the back door, and the firing was loud. Leonard was at work.

I emptied a clip, and while I was reloading one of those Manny had given me, I dropped down behind the alley for protection, and when I did, splinters from the alley floor in front of the loading rack were knocked up by wild shots. Some of the splinters sprayed me. One of them stuck in my cheek, another in my forehead.

I crawled along the floor with my weapons, holding the long gun, the pistols shoved into my coat pockets. I was pushing the shotgun before me. All those shells in my pockets made me feel as heavy as a bag of bricks.

I inched down two lanes, came up there, poked the rifle through, let loose again. This time I caught someone coming in the front door, probably thinking he was safe, that I was pinned down and couldn't shoot.

He was wrong.

I cut him across the groin with one sweep, across the neck with another as he dropped to a knee. I thought I saw some sparks against his chest, where shots had hit his protective vest. The shooter fell over against the headless shadow already there, and I could hear him moaning, and it was a sickening sound. I wanted to shoot him again just to shut him up but knew I should save the ammunition. That guy, alive or not, was fucked, and good, and he was no longer a threat.

Leonard was breaking it down, shooting fast, flooding the back door like a fireman watering flames. After a moment, the firing stopped. It was clear Leonard had driven them back. I heard him click in a new clip.

We hadn't been as easy as they'd thought, not the way we were positioned. They thought we were cake, and we were poison.

Come on, motherfuckers, come on back, run at it again.

I felt the fire rising up in me. I felt the thing I feared about myself most. A kind of anger that could surface and make me red-hot and madly savage or coldly efficient; sometimes, it was a little of both. It was a thing that squirmed in the primitive part of my brain. It came loose a little too easy, but right then, I needed it. I was down to survival, not philosophy.

I didn't know how much was in the new clip, because the first one went pretty fast. I had held the trigger down on that one, like my finger was glued to it. I decided I had to be more careful. The shotgun was near me and I had the handguns. They were backup, but my best bet right then was the military-style weapon from the cop-shop armory.

I dropped back out of sight, my ears open for any sound. After a moment, it was all too much, and I slipped up for a peek.

No one was moving. The moaning was still going on. And then there was a burst and a bright burn of gunfire stitched across the night and the moaner was put out of his misery. They had killed their own killer.

That was one way to do it. At least it was quiet for a moment.

I knew one thing: Mercy from them was not an option, not if they cleaned up their wounded like that. I had a feeling when it came down to us it wouldn't be that quick. No way.

Wilson Keith was a vengeful asshole. He was going to make it as miserable for us as he could manage.

I was trying not to breathe too loudly, but my breath was still a little ragged. It felt as if it were climbing out of my lungs wearing a sandpaper suit.

Leonard opened up again, fire jumping from his position. I heard the sound of hot lead smacking flesh and bone.

And then there was a ramming noise and the back wall moved, and then there was a crashing sound, and some of the ceiling came down behind me.

Keith's vehicle had slammed into the back door of the bowling alley, pushed forward, and stopped. I could see the nose of it. The tires rotated savagely. Keith's killer machine was stuck; it had broken the doorway apart, but the back end had hung up somehow. I could tell that by the black smoke wafting up from the front tires. There was a cracking sound, and the vehicle edged in a little more, its headlights bright, its row of lights on the roof brighter. The tires grabbed the floor and the truck broke completely free of the wall and came charging into the room like a bull looking to gore a matador.

A window was down on the driver's side, and a long gun was hanging out of it, and it was firing in Leonard's direction. Leonard jumped behind the wall, out of sight. The truck stopped and the driver got out holding his weapon.

It wasn't Keith. It was the big black guy.

The weapon in his hand looked like something out of a science fiction movie. He was crouched and ready, but he wasn't firing.

Then there was a loud blast followed by a crash and a tin-kling of glass. The light from the vehicle was so bright that even though the big man was not in front of it, I could still see him clearly in its spreading glow, and in that moment, when the glass fell from on high, the top of the big man's head split wide open and his knees folded and he hit the floor with one leg twisted behind him in a way no one could nat-urally make his legs go, not even that kung fu son of a bitch, wherever he was.

I glanced up. I saw Manny briefly, she having been the one who'd made the shot that shattered the glass upstairs and split the big guy's head wide open. She darted into the shadows with her gun in her hand. The gunfire from the other side of the vehicle that was sprayed up there was way too late. They had lost one of their best men, and Manny was still an active shooter.

During all the confusion, with the glass shattering, Leonard had moved off the stairs and behind the low wall near the couches. There was a gap there so bowlers could make their way to the bathroom, get better shoes, or cross over to the vending-machine room. I discovered he was there be-cause suddenly he was firing from that position, and whoever was at the vehicle wasn't firing back.

Leonard crossed from his spot toward the vehicle. At the same time, two people came through the front door; one went right, the other left. I shot the one on the left as cleanly as if he had been nailed to the floor waiting for it; it was an-other head shot. Like us, they all wore vests. Bullets we had might penetrate those, but I wasn't taking any chances now. I was no longer a butcher. I was a surgeon.

The one on the right was coming up behind Leonard, ducking along the low wall. I wanted to yell out at Leonard but didn't. I didn't want to alert the guy to where I was, because it was my guess he didn't know I was there. Seeing Leonard was just too much for him, like a hound after a rabbit. Worse, I couldn't see Leonard anymore, but I was pretty sure the shooter would be able to see him near the vehicle that had broken through the wall. Wherever our bad guy lifted up from behind the wall to fire at Leonard, I had to be ready. I began to sweat like a goat at a barbecue.

That's when there was another shot from upstairs. More glass rained down and I saw a rifle fly up from behind the short wall and knew Manny had nailed him.

Bless you, Manny.

I crawled through the opening in the pin rack, pushing the rifle in front of me, pulling the shotgun behind me.

I heard shots where Leonard had gone, near the vehicle, and I went there, discarding the rifle and carrying the shotgun with me, anticipating close work. When I got there, a dead woman was on the floor, the one I had seen with Keith back at the police station. Her face had been moved from left to right, or maybe it was right to left; it was such a mess, you couldn't really tell.

Leonard was standing there, looking pretty calm considering the circumstances.

"Okay?" I said.

"Yep," Leonard said. "You?"

"So far, but I may need you to wipe my ass later."

We were looking around all the time, watching for Keith or any remaining minions. I'm sure we both expected Kung Fu Bobby to show up eventually. I plucked the splinters from my face and flicked them away. I was trembling a little. I no longer felt warm. Now I could feel the cold air and it made me cold, and the wind from outside was ruffling my hair like an excited girlfriend.

I opened the door on the vehicle and looked inside. There was no one there. The motor was running and it was warm inside with the heater on, and the overhead light was bright enough you could damn near see the air crawl. There was a scoped rifle of some sort in the seat, and I had never seen such a weapon. It was silver in color and the stock was thick and the scope on it looked large and cumbersome, but when I picked the gun up, it was as light as a poor man's wallet. I took a moment to look through the scope. It was a nightscope and you could see shapes clearly in it, though all of them looked slightly alien and gold-colored.

I kept the rifle and leaned the shotgun against the truck, closed the door. We each took a side of the vehicle and made our way through the debris it had created when it slammed through the wall. Outside, in the wind and the rain, we didn't see anyone. I pulled the hood up on my slicker, and the rain rattled against it. Then we heard the SUV out front start up. We rushed back inside, and we could see headlights shine in through the open front door, and the lights began to move

226

away, like two small, bright moons falling off a cliff. The SUV was backing out of the drive, down the rise of the road.

Now we knew where Kung Fu Bobby and Keith were. They were hightailing it out of there.

"Jump in," Leonard said.

He rushed back to the armored vehicle, climbed in behind the wheel. I was about to climb in on the passenger side when I looked up and saw Manny standing at the edge of where the glass wall had been. Nikki was beside her. They were both holding handguns.

"Get him," Manny said.

I got in, carrying the rifle I had taken and the shotgun too. Leonard backed us out with the vehicle making a lion-like roar, taking some of the remaining back door and wall with it for a few yards, and then he turned the wheel to the left, and away we went, around the back of the bowling center, around the side of it, and down the driveway, which had already been navigated by the SUV.

When we reached the highway, we knew which way they had gone, because the road to Tyler was blocked. Unless they had managed to come up with a cloak of invisibility or the SUV had the ability to fly away into the wet, windy blackness of night, they had to have headed back toward LaBorde.

Leonard yelled out, "Giddyup, Scout."

43

The security vehicle had swift and powerful windshield wipers. They slapped the rain away with the speed of a hummingbird's wings. The lights were phenomenal, cutting through the wet dark effortlessly. Our roaring ride began to catch up with the black SUV, its taillights revealed in our head beams.

A moment later we were riding their ass. Leonard bumped them lightly, then hit them harder. The SUV began to spin, and the wet streets made it worse. Leonard slowed, and the SUV wobbled to the side of the road as a tire blew and then it went skipping left toward a deep roadside ditch and a line of dark trees that were in front of a fenced-in pasture. I could see clearly because the morning light was beginning to slip through the sky.

The SUV's tires shed rubber like a snakeskin, and the

rubber slammed against the windshield of our stolen killer machine and flapped away without so much as leaving a mark.

We had passed the SUV by then; it had stopped when it jumped the ditch, went off into the trees, and smacked against a big sweet gum. It had turned sideways, but not before a door had come open and dumped the contents of people out of it as fast as shit flying out a diarrheic goose.

Leonard stopped slowly, then turned Scout—as I now affectionately thought of the armored vehicle—around and headed back where the SUV had gone off into the line of trees.

He pulled to the side of the road and angled Scout a little so that the headlights and the overhead spots illuminated the scene.

We could see both Keith and Kung Fu Bobby climbing up out of the water-filled ditch. Kung Fu Bobby was up and gone into the woods so fast, I wasn't even sure I had seen him. Keith had lost his hat and ran out of steam. He clutched at the far side of the ditch, but the mud came away in his hands and he slid backward like a slug on teflon.

It was a deep ditch. The rushing water in it came up to his waist and it was moving him around. He caught hold of some roots sticking out of the side of the ditch and clung to them.

I pulled the rifle off the seat, and we got out. Leonard had the shotgun with him. I climbed on top of Scout's cab. I looked through the scope at the tops of the trees, and then I stood up on the cab and looked some more. I could see the trees and the fence and the field from up there, and the scope outlined Kung Fu Bobby climbing between the wires of the barbed-wire fence, then running like a goddamn cheetah across that field.

The wind was stout, and it was all I could do to stand there and not be blown off. I could feel it lashing my hair, so I knew from which direction it was coming and in which direction it would push my bullet. I judged the speed of the wind instinctively, guessed about how fast it would move my shot. I had killed others this night, and before, but this was different. I was homing in on a living human that couldn't harm me now and who was running away and had his back to me.

I hesitated.

And then I took a deep breath and kept Kung Fu Bobby outlined in the scope. I pulled my aim a little to the right, accommodating the blowing of the wind, and elevated the barrel slightly. I slowly let out my breath and gently tugged on the trigger. Kung Fu Bobby looked like part of a video game in the scope and that bothered me even more.

He tried to kill you and Leonard and Nikki, I told myself. He would kill you now if he thought he had the advantage. He might have been the one that killed the lady in the hospital. He certainly helped make it possible. He may be human, but he lacks humanity.

I told myself this as I looked through the scope, the very essence of inhumanity to man on my mind. I was surprised when the shot fired. The sound of it startled me a little, like when the proctologist finally sticks his greased finger up your ass.

I had missed. I had misjudged the rain and the wind. The shot carried past him and hit on his left side and I could see a small jump of dirt in the scope. I pushed my shot a little farther right. He was getting close to the barbed-wire fence on the far side, another line of trees. I had only a few seconds.

Still, take your time, I told myself. Don't get in a hurry.

I lifted the barrel slightly higher. I could barely see him in the scope, as I was having to give up so much of his view for the wind and the carrying of the bullet.

Once again, when the rifle fired, I was startled, but this time I saw Kung Fu Bobby stagger a little, go to one knee, come up again. By now he had reached the barbed-wire fence. He was slipping between two strands of it when he quit moving and collapsed on the bottom strand, like an oversize bird on a telephone wire. He lay still, his arms and legs dangling, and then he rolled off the wire toward the tree line. Only his left foot was still on the wire.

I took a deep breath, tried not to congratulate myself on being an efficient killer. I climbed down from the roof of the truck, went down the side of the road to the edge of the ditch.

Leonard was squatted there. He had laid the shotgun across his knees. I could hear Keith talking when I came up.

"There's no reason you should have won that firefight," he said. "None."

"Ain't life funny," Leonard said. "Reason we won is our secret weapon. Right, Hap?"

"That's right," I said. "We used the elephant of surprise."

"Listen here. I could use boys like you. And I mean for front work, lots of money."

"Do you have dental in your plan?" I said.

"Listen, now, I'm making a serious offer."

"And I'm going to give you a serious answer," Leonard said. "First part of that answer is you've done bad to a lot of people, and I'm sure you'll do more bad if I give you the chance. And the rest of the answer is even more simple: I see that gun you're reaching for."

Keith had been reaching, talking, distracting, looking for his moment, and he'd thought he had us.

Leonard swiveled the shotgun off his knees, and, still squatting, he shot Keith in the head, taking most of it away. Keith's gun fell out of his hands and into the water, and then Keith slipped down the slope and was caught up in a clog of brush for a moment. The flowing water moved the brush away from him, and he eased the rest of the way down. His body tumbled over a couple of times due to the power of the water, and then hung up in some exposed roots on the side of the ditch and stayed there, his feet swaying in the water but going nowhere. Parts of his head on the side of the ditch dripped down too. I could see this clearly because the sun was coming up red as a plum, and the wind was beginning to blow out and the rain went with it.

44

When we got back to the side of the road, a figure came crawling out of the damaged SUV. It surprised us. We thought everyone inside had been thrown out. He stood and put his hands up.

"Hey, guys, don't shoot. I don't want nothing to do with this shit anymore." His hair was washed down over his forehead and he looked as pathetic as a drowning rat.

"You've decided to retire a little late," I said.

"I'm Larry Keith. Law wants me. For God's sake, take me to the law. Don't shoot me. Please don't shoot."

Leonard studied him. "Why not?"

"Because I want to talk. I want to tell everything I know about my father and his work. I want a deal. Was one of those shots . . . him?"

"Yep," Leonard said.

Larry looked toward the ditch. I doubted he could see his old man from that angle, but he looked for a long moment anyway.

"I didn't even like him and he didn't really like me, and still I feel bad. Good God. We used to go to the zoo."

"I hope you got to see the monkeys," Leonard said, "because you won't be going to the zoo again anytime soon. You'll be living in one."

The way Larry stood there, the way his head was hung, his wet hair in his face, his hands lifted, I felt bad for him. There was no reason to feel that way, but I did. Right then I felt bad about everything.

We found some rope in the back of the truck, tied Larry up with it, loaded him in the vehicle, bound him to the passenger seat. Leonard drove him and us back to the bowling center.

As we went, the red sun rose higher, and the thin mist in the trees began to melt. I saw birds flying over the tops of the trees, and before we had gone far, the red sun became gold, and the sky was absent of clouds and had turned a bright baby-blanket blue.

45

I felt sad about Kung Fu Bobby, more than the others, until they went out to get his body and he wasn't there. That helped me out, in a way, because I didn't have to explain shooting him as he was running away. Not to anyone, even myself.

They looked where I'd said he was, and then they looked in the tree line and beyond, but they didn't find him. He hadn't got up wounded and wandered off and died. They didn't find any blood.

I knew then I had missed twice. Unusual for me. Maybe in the back of my mind I meant to miss. And maybe it was the rain and the wind. I don't know. But Kung Fu Bobby had fooled me, had taken a dive into that fence, and, in his acrobatic way, he had been convincing.

He was out there somewhere.

Larry Keith turned out to be a big ol' blabbermouth and he told everything, admitted he saw the murder of Pretty Boy but tried to distance himself from it, like it wasn't his idea at all, that he was just an observer, not the one who pulled the trigger. He knew singing loud and clear might give him a reduced sentence. It wasn't all that reduced. Twenty years. Not what he deserved, but what he got.

Nikki, when her tongue was well, gave her testimony, and if Old Man Keith had been alive, he'd have gotten the death penalty. Well, he got it anyway.

Leonard and I were cleared of any charges. Manny made us out to be heroes, and I guess we were. I hope we were. Thinking of it that way helps me sleep at night.

LaBorde was devastated by the storm. Downtown had stood pretty well, but along the streets and out in the country, the hurricane winds, the tornado spin-offs, and the high water had destroyed a lot.

We got declared a national disaster area, and already the town is rebuilding. That's the Texas way. We might have our faults, but we can get shit done if someone throws a barbecue with it.

Leonard's apartment fared fine, and so did our office, though the bicycle shop below us was washed out. Somewhere a large perch is riding a ten-speed.

Mine and Brett's house was easy enough to repair, and we had that done right away, thanks to the insurance, and after a few months had passed and Kung Fu Bobby hadn't shown up, I decided he had moved on. Practical. He wasn't the kind of guy, at least in my estimation, to stick to an agenda that wasn't paying. His loyalty was to the hire, not the man. I wondered where he was right then, what he was thinking. Probably learning to leap tall buildings in a single bound.

Wondering doesn't give much in the way of results, though. Months later I would still be wondering, though with less frequency.

Nikki came out fine, and when our house was repaired, we had a house-repair party, and she was invited. She came over wearing a wide-brimmed hat, a pretty yellow dress dotted with blue flowers, little tennis shoes as white as snow.

It was a bright day and cold, and we had cooked all morning. We had enough food to feed the proverbial army, and we had an army coming over. Besides Nikki, we had Hanson, minus his wife, who hated us, and we had Manny and Cason Statler, and there was Pookie, Chance, Reba, and Buffy the Dog, wearing a red-and-white neckerchief and new dog tags, and there was Leonard, of course.

The food was pulled pork and greens and cabbage, and there were hot dogs and hamburgers, fried chicken, dips and chips, and drinks of all kinds. And primarily for Leonard, there was banana pudding with vanilla cookies mixed into it. It was the one dish Reba had made.

We pushed the couch and the furniture in the living room aside, and in the kitchen, we added a foldout table and chairs, and at around two p.m. we attacked the food.

There was lots of talk and laughter, and that helped the

storm and the killing seem distant and long gone and unlikely again. Manny said the city was giving me and Leonard some kind of award for helping law enforcement in a unique time of need. That was about as surprising as discovering a thousand-dollar bill in one of my socks.

Reba was really taken with Nikki's whiteness. She said, "You white as I am black."

Nikki stared at her, said, "But I burn easy and I'm not as pretty as you."

The color of Reba's skin didn't allow us to see her blush, but we could sure sense it in the way her eyes fell and her head turned.

"I ain't pretty."

"Yes, you are. But you might think about working on your hair a bit. I can help you with that later, if you like."

"I don't know."

"It's no trouble."

"You know about my kind of hair?"

"I might surprise you with what I know about hair of all sorts."

"Maybe," Reba said. "Where you get that hat?"

"Goodwill."

"Nah, you didn't."

"Did."

"Be damn. Looks like it high-end."

"It was at one time. But at Goodwill, it was my price."

When the talk became repetitive, Brett, beautiful in jeans and a black T-shirt and red slip-on shoes, pushed her long red hair back and bound it, turned on the CD player, put one on and others to follow.

"Runaround Sue" by Dion came up first, and Brett held out her hand to me while swaying her hips from side to side. It was an invitation impossible to ignore. I came in from the kitchen and took her hand.

She said, "Hap, let's dance, baby."

I used to dance well, but I didn't do it much anymore. But right then that music was beautiful and stirring, and I began to dance, and my body became loose and easy. I told myself I would never pick up a gun again. I would never get involved with anything where I might be hurt or I might hurt someone else. It wasn't the first time I had spoken to myself that way.

Brett dropped my hand and came in close and we rolled our shoulders and swung our hips, touched noses, then moved back and let the music take us.

Reba laughed, but then she and Nikki were out there with us, dancing together, clowning a little. Cason and Manny joined in, followed by Pookie and Leonard.

Leonard proved once again that the idea that all black men can dance is a myth. He had the rhythm of a broken clock. But Pookie, now, he had it, man. He could move.

Hanson kept his seat and clapped his hands to the beat.

Brett signaled to him, did it a couple of times. Hanson got up and came over. She grabbed his shirt and pulled him close and the three of us danced until Hanson's bad leg sent him back to his chair.

More old music followed, the Beach Boys, early Beatles,

Buddy Holly, the Sun hits of Johnny Cash, all the gods of rhythm and blues, rockabilly, and rock 'n' roll. Brett turned it up.

As we danced, the day began to fade and the night began to crawl and the room turned dark.

Hanson turned on the lights. We all stopped and ate some more, had some coffee while some slow ones played, and then we were back at it when the fast ones came, dancing like fools. We did that tirelessly, late into the night, constantly re-placing played-out sounds with unplayed sounds, and at some point, for no reason I could determine, there were tears in my eyes, running down my cheeks.

I looked at Brett and smiled, and she smiled back.

Joe R. Lansdale is the author of nearly four dozen novels, including *Jackrabbit Smile, Edge of Dark Water,* the Edgar Award–winning *The Bottoms,* and the Spur Award–winning *Paradise Sky.* He has received eleven Bram Stoker Awards, the American Mystery Award, the British Fantasy Award, and the Grinzane Cavour Prize. He lives with his family in Nacogdoches, Texas.

MULHOLLAND BOOKS

You won't be able to put down these Mulholland books.

....

KILLING EVE: NO TOMORROW *by Luke Jennings*

THE ELEPHANT OF SURPRISE *by Joe R. Lansdale*

CROWN JEWEL *by Christopher Reich*

TOMBLAND *by C. J. Sansom*

SEAL TEAM SIX: HUNT THE LEOPARD *by Don Mann and Ralph Pezzullo*

DECEPTION COVE *by Owen Laukkanen*

CONVICTION *by Denise Mina*

THE CHAIN *by Adrian McKinty*

THE GOMORRAH GAMBIT *by Tom Chatfield*

PLAY WITH FIRE *by William Shaw*

SAVIORS: TWO NOVELS *by Malcolm Mackay*

....